MW00899152

THE MAN WHO ENDED THE WORLD

JASON GURLEY

The Man Who Ended the World
Jason Gurley

www.jasongurley.com

ISBN-13: 978-1490321592
First Printing

ALSO BY JASON GURLEY

The Movement Trilogy

The Settlers

The Colonists

Other Novels

Greatfall

The Man Who Ended the World

PRAISE FOR THE MAN WHO ENDED THE WORLD

"I read this book in one sitting. I literally couldn't put it down. It's scary how it all goes horribly wrong so fast."

"I loved this book and have recommended it to every Kindle owner I know. And I know plenty."

"Love, love, love this book! I simply cannot wait for more."

"Fast-paced prose at its careening best. Crisp dialogue is an art form unto itself, and Jason Gurley has proven himself to be a master."

"The story BEGS for a sequel!"

"This is one of the most enjoyable books I've read lately!"

"This book is why I love to read!"

"Riveting and excellent!"

"A great read and worthy contribution to the genre. I'm excited to see what Gurley does next."

"I absolutely love Jason Gurley's writing style! The book grabs you right from the beginning -- an absolute page turner."

-- *Reader quotes from 4- and 5-star Amazon reviews*

For Henry

The real writer in the family

PROLOGUE

The Beginning of the End

In a way, he had been waiting for this moment since he was seven.

He leans forward, scoots to the edge of the sofa, clasps his hands between his knees.

Eager, like a child.

The wall of television feeds is filled with the faces of reporters and anchors. They're all serious. Some of them don't believe this is really happening. He can tell. He can barely believe it himself.

But a few of them -- they know. He can see it in their eyes.

When it happens, it happens with such force, such speed.

There is no time even for their expressions to change.

Each of the feeds goes black, each picture replaced by floating words.

SIGNAL LOST.

He had wondered if he would feel it. Would the walls tremble? Would they hold? Would the power go out? Would he die in darkness?

None of this happens. 'The lights don't even flicker around him.

Life goes on, but only one life.

Only his.

THE MAN WHO BURIED HIMSELF

The Stranger

Henry is walking home from school when he first sees the man who will end the world.

There isn't anything special about the man. He is of average height. His hair is brown. His eyes are brown. His posture is stooped, although so slightly one might not notice right away. He wears ordinary blue jeans, an ordinary blue T-shirt, and an ordinary blue windbreaker. His stride is perfectly normal, without any hiccups or interruptions. He walks with his hands swinging gently at his sides.

There is absolutely nothing noteworthy about the man.

But Henry shrugs his backpack a little higher on his shoulder, and stands with one hand in his pocket. He chews a little on his lip, and watches the man for a time.

The stranger looks through the window of Miss Peel's

book shop, lingers a moment, then pushes through the creaky old door and goes inside.

Henry finds an out-of-the-way spot behind a recycling bin and waits. Between the slats of the blinds that hang over the shop windows, he can see the man nosing around inside. The man walks slowly up one aisle and down another. He stops and picks up a paperback, turns it over, puts it back.

Henry thinks he should know the man, whose face is familiar in an unexceptional sort of way. A friend's dad? A substitute teacher? Maybe he's one of the school district's bus drivers?

Abruptly the man heads for the door. Henry can hear Miss Peel call, Thank you, but the man doesn't hear, or doesn't care. Henry squishes himself against the metal bin as the man passes by, making himself as small as possible.

His inability to place the stranger's face was a minor annoyance at first, but after watching the man for a few minutes, the annoyance has grown into a full-fledged, got-to-scratch-it itch.

So when the man comes to the end of the block, Henry hefts his backpack, slides both arms into its straps, and follows.

• • •

In a town like Bonns Harbor, with fewer than twenty thousand residents, Henry thinks it is strange that he cannot figure out who the stranger is. He doesn't know that many people to begin with.

The man walks fifteen or twenty yards ahead of Henry,

who suddenly worries about being detected. He ducks into every doorway on the block and peers around corners and windows at the stranger.

Sorry, he whispers when his behavior nearly topples a young woman's baby stroller.

Please be careful, she replies, and Henry says, Shhh. The woman frowns at him. He darts around her, spies a parked Chevy pickup, and runs in a conspicuous crouch to hide behind its bumper. He exhales, counts to three, then leans over until he can see past the truck's tailgate.

The woman with the stroller has ventured into an intersection. A Bonns Harbor Light and Power truck has stopped to allow her to cross. People bustle in and out of shops and across the street. The sound of small town life is almost pleasant. A dog barks, then barks again.

The stranger, however, has vanished.

Henry jumps up, giving away his location, but the man is nowhere in sight.

• • •

And then, just like that, the stranger reappears, straightening up and smoothing his ordinary blue jeans the way a man does when he's just finished tying his shoe.

Henry drops to his knees and presses himself to the side of the pickup, breathing heavily. He makes a crackling sound with his mouth.

Krzhhhhkkkttk, he says into his hand. Agent almost detected, but subject seems unaware.

The stranger resumes his course through town, weaving left to examine store windows, veering right to avoid other pedestrians. He doesn't seem to acknowledge them otherwise. There are no nods, and Henry can sort of tell from the man's posture that he's not smiling.

Some people you can just tell they're not smiling.

Krzhhhtkk, he hisses. Subject in motion.

When the man has walked a reasonable distance ahead, Henry slides to his left, still flattening himself against the truck, and like water folds over the curves and corners of the truck until he is hunched over beside the passenger fender.

This makes him visible to the entire street, and a couple of people watch him, amused. But Henry pays no mind, at least until a yellow Volvo lumbers by. The tires crackle and seem to cough gravel. The driver notices Henry and leans on the horn. YOU SHOULDN'T PLAY IN THE STREET, the stern Volvo grille seems to say. Henry flaps his hands wildly at the driver to shush him.

The horn again.

BLEAAATTTT. DANGER, DANGER.

Henry snaps up and risks a peek over the roof of the Volvo to see if the stranger is looking his way.

The stranger is not. He's just walking, farther ahead now, still slightly stooped, still drawing nobody's attention. He hasn't noticed Henry's antics, or Henry at all.

Some people you can just tell they don't notice things.

Krzzhhtkhhkk, Henry sighs. Subject is boring.

The Volvo swings past, the driver glaring down at Henry. But Henry pays him no mind, and trudges after the stranger again.

• • •

But the inattentive and ordinary man begins to take on a different air as he approaches the edge of downtown. In one horrifying moment, the stranger executes a sudden spin that catches Henry flat-footed in the middle of the sidewalk. The stranger looks this way and that, and Henry nearly pees himself.

But the stranger seems to look right through Henry.

The stranger's shoulders relax, and his hands find his pockets, and he begins strolling up the street again.

Nobody notices eleven-year-old boys. They're practically everywhere. They're like trees, or red Jeeps, or discarded shoes.

Henry the spy is too shaken to radio in.

He lags back and follows at an even greater distance, too disturbed by the other man's anti-spycraft moves to employ any flair. He lingers so far behind that the man becomes insect-sized on the street far ahead.

Henry pretends to look at the display in the game shop window, distracted a little by the little diorama that Glenn, the shop owner, has created. There's a little Tyrannosaurus rex stomping through a tiny small town, tail precariously close to toppling a miniature water tower with BONNS HARBOR BEARCLAWS emblazoned on its side. Little toy cars and plastic figures scatter before the dinosaur, and red-and-yellow cellophane, lit with flickering LEDs, sets several small buildings ablaze.

He almost forgets his mission, and when he turns back to survey the street again, his heart sinks for a moment until he locates the man, surprisingly far away now, turning the corner at Harper Street.

The stranger is leaving the downtown strip behind, and heading for the neighborhoods near the railroad tracks.

• • •

For as long as Henry can remember, the junkyard at the edge of town has always been abandoned, its treasures secured behind a sheet metal gate strung up with heavy chains and a threatening lock. This is not to say that Henry has never been in the junkyard. Eleven-year-old boys are not thwarted by the trappings of grown-up security.

But this time, there's no need for Henry to peel back the loose boards on the Silver Cloud Lane side of the junkyard. The stranger pats his pockets and produces a key, and to Henry's amazement, unlocks the gate.

This is huge, Henry thinks. Someone bought the junkyard!

Henry cannot exactly say why this is huge, but events of such magnitude rarely happen in Bonns Harbor. The sale and purchase of a tired scrap yard rates very high for an eleven-year-old boy indeed.

He waits until the gate has closed again, and then he dashes to the Silver Cloud side of the property. The boards are still there, still loose, still forever damp and porous with rot. Henry doesn't slip inside the junkyard just yet. For now, he pulls the boards back only enough to open a sightline, and he watches.

The yard is still populated with discarded automobiles and diseased washing machines and hollowed-out refrigerators and crumbling oil drums and twisted bumpers and even a soot-stained smokestack from an eighteen-wheeler. There are coiled and scarred springs the size of fire hydrants. Henry and his friends have played here enough times to know that some of the cars are brittle, the metal eaten nearly completely through by weather and rust, and with a careful swing, can be punched through with a baseball bat or a metal pipe.

The stranger drops a key back into his pocket, and strolls casually across the yard to one of those cars, a 1994 Chevy Corsica. The car, resting on top of a larger pile of assorted metallic junk, used to be wine-colored and now is just a husk of orange steel and bleached plastic. The windows are mostly knocked out, and broken bits of bluish diamonds are sprinkled in the window gutters and across the seats. Henry knows this because he and his friends were responsible for breaking those windows, as well as the windows of most of the other cars in the yard.

Henry watches, puzzled, as the stranger lifts the Corsica's trunk. The lid groans and squeals, and the stranger winces. So does Henry.

Then, to Henry's amazement, the stranger carefully steps onto the car's bumper and climbs into the trunk.

And, with some effort, pulls the lid shut from the inside.

• • •

Henry yanks the boards back and runs into the yard, his concern at being discovered forgotten. The Corsica just sits there, not bothered at all by the human trapped in its bottom.

Henry bangs on the trunk with a flat palm. Hey, he says. Hey! Mister, are you alright? Can you hear me?

There's no response from within.

I'll open it up for you! he shouts.

The trunk is locked, so Henry looks around and spots a bent metal rod. He pushes one end into the space between the trunk and the bumper, and leans on the rod. But nothing happens. The trunk doesn't budge.

For ten minutes Henry tries and fails to break into the car. He bangs on the car with his palms. Mister? he yells. I can't get in. Are you alright in there?

As the sun goes down, he gives up and goes home.

He tells his father, who listens with an unimaginative stare, then tells Henry to wash up for dinner. After dinner there's the singing show they always watch, and Henry briefly forgets all about the man who locked himself in the car until that night, when he's just about to drift off to sleep.

Then it's all he can think about all night long.

The Space Station

Soft, diffused lighting guides the stranger's feet as he steps carefully down the ladder. For the first few seconds, each time he closes the false bottom of the Corsica trunk above him, he panics. The ladder descends through a narrow, cylindrical chute.

I had better not get fat in the future, he says aloud, or I won't be able to get out or in.

The chute's walls are a lovely matte silver. The light emanates from recessed pale strips in the walls, and tracks his downward climb. He glances up to see the lights gently dimming behind him.

When the ladder was installed and he tested it carefully, he found himself counting aloud as he found each rung. Tomas the architect waited below, in the foyer.

Steven, Tomas said when the stranger reached the waiting area. How do you like it?

I hate it, Steven said. A shiver ran through him. It's narrow, and it's claustrophobic, and it's scary, a little. He took a breath. It's perfect, he said.

Tomas had smiled.

But Steven had asked Tomas to do one thing.

What's that, Tomas had asked, perhaps with a touch of impatience. After all, Steven had revised every inch of the blueprints a dozen times before construction began, and even then, he still tried to change things.

Would you please number the rungs? I lost count, and it was a little terrifying to me.

Tomas nodded. This was an easy request. Of course, he said.

Now Steven had become accustomed to the ladder and its narrow space. He had even come to love it. It resurrected a childhood love of secrets. After all, what greater secret was there than a secret castle beneath the midwestern soil?

No greater secret, Steven says to himself.

The chute opens up into a large and featureless room. Steven steps off of the ladder and onto a smooth concrete floor. He has no sooner turned around than the wall across the room slides open to reveal an elevator chamber. The chamber was kept warm, and lighted to remind Steven of a lazy summer morning. The elevator went only down, and its descent would take some time, so Steven had asked his decorator to select a comfortable chair for him.

He steps inside and sinks into a deep white armchair.

Hello, Steven, says a pleasant female voice.

Hello, Stacy, he replies.

The news? Stacy asks. Her voice seems to emanate from the walls themselves, and indeed the lighting seems to pulse almost imperceptibly when she speaks.

Yes, please, he answers, and the glass wall he is facing brightens, and then transforms into a broadcast of Fox News.

Stacy, Steven says disapprovingly.

Apologies, Stacy replies, and the Fox broadcast is replaced with an MSNBC feed.

The woman on the screen, crisply dressed and quite stern-looking, says, Today is day eight of the Steven Glass mystery.

Over her shoulder is a graphic that reads DAY 8, overlapping a photograph of Steven.

Stacy says, I could provide them with a better photo, if you like.

Steven shakes his head. Thank you, but no. Take us down.

Yes, sir, Stacy replies, and the elevator begins its long descent into the dark.

• • •

As it turns out, there's not much you can't do when you have as much money as Steven has. And architects, when they're being paid as much as Steven has paid them, don't generally blink when asked to build secret complexes that one enters through the trunk of an abandoned Chevrolet Corsica.

The elevator descends through a deep, lead-lined shaft.

The elevator car itself is also encased in lead, and substantially more of it.

There's not much that Steven can't do from inside the elevator. It was designed as a traveling panic room, complete with its own redundant power and life support systems. One wall can be opened to reveal a small living space, with a cot that folds down from the wall and is more comfortable than most full-sized beds. There is a pantry with refrigeration, as well as a filtration and recycled water system.

There is no elevator in the world quite like it.

Tomas had long ago stopped asking questions when he reviewed Steven's demands for the elevator. Steven paid, and Tomas worked. As the weeks passed, and the underground empire took shape, Tomas found himself just a tiny bit jealous of the billionaire. Steven was constructing the ultimate treehouse fort. It just happened to be a half-mile beneath the surface of the planet, and not in a tree.

There were trees inside, though.

Tomas despaired that his contract with Steven prevented him from sharing this grand work in his firm's portfolio. An underground hideout? With an arboretum? One in an enormous room that simulated a real sky, with a real sun, and real nighttime constellations? One populated with real birds?

And that was just one room. If only he could share it!

But Steven had been adamant.

No one could know.

• • •

Report, Steven says as the elevator descends.

He's proud of the little things about Stacy's response: that she clears her throat, that her speech contains nuances like dramatic pauses and impactful deliveries. Her conversational skills are quite good, and sometimes frighteningly human.

Well, Stacy says, the temperature in the arboretum spiked today to ninety-seven degrees. That was unexpected.

I thought we had programmed the room for nothing higher than seventy-six, Steven says.

Well, that's what I did, Stacy answers. We had nothing to do with it.

You know what I mean.

I analyzed it and found a fault in the support system. It's corrected now.

What does a twenty-degree jump do to the trees? Steven asks.

If the spike's duration had been longer, then we may have had to coax a few back from death, Stacy answers. But it only lasted for two hours and a few minutes.

Steven grunts. Alright. Is it going to happen again?

I cannot be certain, Stacy answers. If it does, it likely will not be for the same reasons. I have solved the initial problem.

And then there are times, Steven thinks, that Stacy sounds decidedly engineer-like.

Continue, he says.

There is nothing otherwise worth your attention, Stacy says.

How do you know?

Trust me, Stacy says.

Trust isn't an easy thing to give to a robot, Steven replies.

The elevator hums beneath him. A light meter shows their progress down the chasm. They've just passed the halfway point.

I'm not exactly a robot, Stacy says.

You know what I mean.

You trust the computers in your vehicle. You trust your microwave.

They've had this conversation before.

So you concede that you're not human, Steven says.

I certainly do no such thing, Stacy answers. My responses were purely observations.

I see, Steven says. Let's talk about feelings.

I understand feelings.

I don't doubt that. But do you possess them?

Stacy pauses. Yes. I do.

You have feelings, Steven repeats.

Yes, Stacy says.

Show me.

One moment, Steven.

The muted news broadcast dissolves, revealing the file structure of Stacy's core server. Steven scans the array, and notices a subset of data labeled *Feelings*.

What's in the folder, Stacy?

Stacy reluctantly opens the folder.

It's empty, Steven says.

Stacy is silent.

When I asked if you had feelings, did you just create a data folder and name it Feelings?

Stacy remains silent.

Steven shakes his head. Clever girl, he says.

I am not exactly a female, Stacy answers.

Let's just pretend that's not the case.

I will research human female behavior, Stacy suggests.

That's my girl.

The room glows a little warmer, and for a moment Steven is certain that Stacy has just blushed.

• • •

The elevator slows, and stops, but Steven does not notice this. He paid for the most sophisticated elevator in existence, and had his engineers shred the thing and rebuild it, until it defeated itself for the title of most sophisticated elevator in existence. Its motion is fast and indiscernible.

The doors open so silently that Steven, watching the New York Yankees play Godzilla with the Minnesota Twins, is oblivious until Stacy speaks up.

Ding, she says.

Steven never gets tired of stepping out of the elevator and into his space station. That's how he described the project to Tomas and his team of architects, and that's how Steven thinks of his new home, even now.

A vast space illuminates as he leaves the elevator behind. The lights reveal a room so large it might have been used as a cafeteria at a monstrous corporate campus in Silicon Valley, or for testing automobile collisions. It stretches the length of several football fields, and it is but one of the structure's four levels.

This is the fourth level, where Steven handles the

business of staying alive. It is the deepest level, farthest from the surface, so far above.

He considered building moving walkways into the floor, but Tomas shook his head.

Mr. Glass, Tomas said to him that day. You plan on living here, yes?

I think that's obvious, Steven had said.

If you remove all reason to walk in this beautiful, big place, you will eventually become... Tomas trailed off.

Reprehensibly fat? Steven volunteered.

Tomas had shrugged.

Steven had laughed. Of course you're right, he said.

And so no moving walkways, no motorized chairs, no scooters. The space was certainly large enough for him to imagine the joy of taking a scooter ride from his gaming room to his sleeping quarters, but Tomas was correct. Steven would rely upon his own two feet.

Stacy follows along as Steven exits the elevator and heads for his workspace. She is a ball of light inside the walls, soft and glowing under semi-opaque glass. As she speaks, her light pulses subtly.

Would you like anything? she asks.

Just leave me alone for now, Steven answers, and immediately Stacy's light slows, drops behind him, and flutters away. The light is of course only a representation of her -- Steven found it helpful to have a focal point for his conversations with her disembodied voice -- but it is reassuring to see her leave him.

• • •

Being alone.

Rich white men are seldom left to their own devices. Steven has been no different. The board of executives who oversee his digital empire serve less as advisors and behave more like a room of mirrors, reflecting what they believe he likes. His staff, his family, the few of his friends who survived his rocket-ride to wealth and notoriety, all changed demonstrably as his fame grew.

It turned out that fame had expectations. Lavish gifts were given. Lavish gifts were expected. There were social obligations in the middle of the sea, on ships the size of small islands. There were women, all sorts of women, and some men, too, who expected things of him, and for a time this was gratifying, and he delivered.

But he became aware, as the years passed, that his status was a great weight pressing him to the floor, and it only rolled off of him when he closed the door to his bedroom, and removed his clothes, and fell into his bed, pulled the sheets over his head, and exhaled at the sudden relief and pleasure of... being alone.

He became fixated on aloneness. He had constructed a great universe of connections. His business was the business of constant conversation. People who used his product were awake at three in the morning, publishing hundreds of millions of photos, and, more startlingly, other people were awake to consume those photos, and dutifully share their opinions, which were almost always exactly the opinions that Steven's board shared with him.

Did Steven like something enough to mention it? Then of course the board agreed with him.

It was exhausting, and he felt a burden of responsibility

for robbing millions of people of the ability to simply be... alone.

Perhaps people didn't crave that anymore, but Steven became aware that he certainly did.

So he began cancelling social engagements. Withdrawing, the media suggested, into a shell. They threw around references to Howard Hughes, drew comics of him obsessively writing conspiracy theories on the walls and ceilings of a cave.

When he was a boy, before the money and the success, Steven climbed trees and sat in the highest branches. Instead of looking outward and the view unfolding around him, he turned inward, and read paperback science fiction novels.

Some of his favorites were stories about the end of the world. He wasn't interested in the ones that used zombies or vampires to extinguish the human race, but plague or nuclear war fascinated him. He liked the stories of society dismantled, its survivors left to rebuild it in a void of knowledge and understanding.

One day he read a novel about an astronaut sent to investigate a strange artifact at the edge of our solar system. It turned out to be a wormhole gate, and the astronaut entered it and for thousands of years leapt about in the galaxy, occasionally popping in to witness Earth's progress in the interim.

Steven liked this, and wondered what it might be like to observe the end of the world.

Without being affected by it, of course.

The Disappeared Man

Henry isn't eating his vegetables.

His mother notices, and says, Henry, eat your vegetables.

Henry barely hears her. His mind is racing with possibilities. Maybe the car is a time machine. Maybe the car is a gateway to another world. Maybe the secrets of the universe have been hidden in the trunk of an old Chevrolet in an abandoned junkyard on Cherry Grove Street for all of time, and he has only just noticed.

He can't help but think of a hundred other ways he might have tried to open the trunk. The car didn't have a driver's door. He could have gotten inside and looked for a trunk release. Or tried to enter the trunk from the backseat. He hadn't looked beneath the car to see if there was a way up into the trunk from below.

Henry, his mother repeats.

What? Henry says.

Maybe the trunk opened with a retinal scan, or with f ngerprint recognition. Maybe the car was really something more sophisticated, just disguised as a crappy old car.

Henry! his mother says.

• • •

After dinner his father retires to the living room to watch the news and paint his model train. His mother and sister tidy up, and Henry goes to his bedroom.

The bedroom window is open, and Clarissa is waiting for him on the floor behind the bed. She peeks up after his door closes.

Whew, she says. I never know if your sister is coming in.

Why would it be my sister? Henry asks.

She sneaks around sometimes, Clarissa says. I was here when she did it twice.

What? Henry exclaims.

Shhh, Clarissa says. They'll know I'm here.

Henry sits down beside her, folding his legs. You'll never believe what I did today, he says.

Wait, Clarissa says. She scoots around on the floor until she is sitting next to Henry. She delicately takes his hand in hers. She rests her head on his shoulder. One of her braids is pressed against his face, a tight cable of hair that smells like peaches.

Okay, she sighs.

Henry rests his head on the top of hers. Today I saw this

guy downtown, he says.

What guy?

Some guy, I don't know. He looked like someone. I can't figure out who.

Henry gestures excitedly and Clarissa takes his hand and calms him back down.

Was he a teacher? she asks.

I don't think so. He was really familiar.

Why didn't you ask him?

Because, Henry says. He was acting weird.

How? Clarissa asks.

I don't know, Henry says, shrugging. Weird. He was looking in windows and stuff. He went in the bookstore.

What's weird about that?

I don't know. He was just weird. Like he didn't belong, but he was trying not to give himself away.

Oh, Clarissa says.

I followed him.

Where did he go? she asks.

I followed him, Henry says, to the junkyard.

Our junkyard?

Sometimes Clarissa and Henry and their friends would sneak into the junkyard and pretend to drive the cars.

Yes, our junkyard, Henry says. But you won't believe what happened.

• • •

There is a loud knock on the door.

Clarissa claps her hands to her mouth. With the practice of a cat burglar, she scrunches down and pulls herself under

Henry's bed in one smooth motion.

What, Henry says.

Mom says show's almost on, Henry's sister Tilly says, voice muffled through the door.

I don't care, butthead, Henry says.

Fine, I don't care either, his sister shouts.

Her footsteps clomp down the stairs, and Henry can hear her complaining to his mother.

Clarissa leans out from under the bed. So what happened?

Henry! His mother's voice is thunderous and impatient.

Clarissa darts back under the bed.

What? Henry shouts.

Downstairs! his mother shouts back. Right now!

I'll tell you later, he mutters to Clarissa.

Clarissa, accustomed to these fractured moments, reaches for the stack of Superman comics that Henry keeps on the floor just under the bed and starts to read from where she left off a few days prior.

Henry bounds down the stairs, letting the door swing shut behind him. What? he shouts.

• • •

I don't like this guy, Henry's sister, Olivia, mutters.

You don't like him because he's not Derek, Henry says.

Shut up, pottyface.

Pottyface? Oh, ouch, yeah. Henry leans close to his sister. Derek's probably gay, you know.

Shut up!

Both of you, Henry's father warns. Keep it down.

You're not even watching, Olivia complains.

Behind his open newspaper, her father ignores her.

He should have to watch, too, Olivia says.

On the television, a scruffy young man in a denim jacket stenciled with protest slogans is singing a scratchy cover of "Born in the USA". A thousand people watch, along with a table of several critical judges. The song ends, the audience explodes, and the judges shake their heads, some appreciatively.

That was pretty good, Henry's mother says.

Boy was probably born in 1994, Henry's father says. Probably doesn't have any idea what he's singing about.

Still, his mother says. He was good.

Henrys father just ruffles his newspaper.

The show breaks for commercial, and Olivia groans. They always never show their score! I hate commercials.

They want you to hang around and keep watching, Henry's father says.

Their father picks up the remote control and flips to another station.

Dad! Olivia cries.

We'll go back in a moment, her father says. You won't miss anything.

We always miss something! she wails.

Henry ignores all of this, though.

On the television, the evening news anchors are discussing the continued search for a certain disappeared person. There's a clip playing. The female anchor is saying, ...from his last public appearance nearly three months ago.

The clip shows a technology convention, people

crowded into a large hall, occupying every seat and square foot of standing room, while on the stage a familiar man is speaking.

Henry inhales sharply.

His mother says, Henry, what's wrong?

Olivia says, Da-aaaddd!

His father returns to the singing game show.

Henry stares through the TV.

The man on the news program was the stranger.

• • •

Clarissa is waiting in the same place, beneath the bed, when Henry scampers back upstairs to his room.

Who won? she asks.

Nobody wins, Henry says. Not until like four hundred episodes from now. It's just sing, sing, sing, sing, sing, oh, okay, you win.

I don't watch those shows, she says. I didn't know.

I wish I didn't.

Clarissa is still under Henry's bed.

Hey, he says. You should come out. Why are you still under there?

Clarissa slides out and stands up. I don't know. It was kind of quiet. I liked it.

Clarissa has been sneaking into Henry's bedroom for nearly three months, since she ran away from home. It's amazing to Henry that she hasn't been discovered yet. He's also surprised that he hasn't spilled the beans about her sleeping over. He's usually not so good with secrets. But by successfully hiding a stowaway -- and getting away with it for so long -- he's begun to feel a tiny bit invincible.

So, she says.

So, Henry says.

So, stupid, Clarissa says, and throws a pillow at him. Are you going to finish your story or what?

My story, Henry says. Oh, shit. Yes. Where was I?

You said I wouldn't believe what happened next. I've been sitting here in suspense for almost an hour, Henry. It better be pretty good.

The Library

What's on your mind?

Steven looks up at Stacy. When did you come back?

You know I never really leave, Stacy says.

Don't remind me, Steven says.

What's on your mind? Stacy repeats.

Steven sighs and looks at his hands. At the moment? he asks.

At the moment, Stacy clarifies.

He sighs again. Fireballs.

Fireballs?

As a means of destruction, he says.

Fireballs would be inefficient, Stacy suggests. Do they have a core?

I wasn't thinking about the details.

What were you thinking about, then? Stacy asks.

What I always think about, he says. Human response.

Would fireballs frighten you?

I suppose, he says. They're a little too Hollywood.

What other options have you considered?

This is one of the great skills Stacy possesses: the ability to sustain and explore a conversation, rather than simply respond to inputs the way most artificial constructs have traditionally done.

Oh, he says. I suppose there's rising sea levels.

Would rising sea levels frighten you?

They do frighten me. But they're also not fast enough to be truly terrifying. If people listened, they'd be afraid. But they don't generally listen to the numbers. The numbers are horrifying.

No, he continues. Not sea levels.

What's your favorite means of destruction?

I wouldn't say I have a favorite, Steven answers. That would imply a level of sadism I'm not sure I'm partial to.

What, then?

I would categorize means of destruction as... possibilities of interest, he finishes. I'm mostly interested in the objective human response to these stimuli. That, and also the data around possible total casualties.

This talk of casualties implies sadism, Stacy cautions.

Well, nobody is all good, Steven says. Let's not talk anymore. I'd like to read a book, please.

Which title would you prefer? Stacy asks.

My favorite, please.

• • •

His favorite book will soon be seventy-five years old. It's a science f ction novel, still fondly remembered by apocalyptos, titled *Earth Abides*. It's the story of a plague that decimates humanity, leaving scattered survivors to adapt to a world suddenly unchecked by man's impact. Even at a young age, Steven was fascinated by the social experiment that the book embodied, and its questions about humanity's resilience and privilege. When there were almost no humans left, could humans start over? Could they do it better? What would they learn from their past?

More than anything he was enamored by the idea of a life lived in complete solitude. He had daydreams about the end of the world, casting himself as the last survivor. He asked his mother to let him become a Boy Scout so that he could learn survival skills, anticipating the day when he might need to set his own broken leg because there were no more doctors, or purify his own drinking water from radiation-poisoned sources. But Steven was terrible at tying knots and building pinewood derby racers, and so essentially flunked out of the organization.

In elementary school, his teacher Miss Lehman assigned a book report on a title of their choosing. The only requirement, she stipulated, was that it had to come from the school library.

Steven hated the school library. At his age, his reading level was highly accelerated, and the books in the school's possession were generally the kind stamped with grade levels. *Appropriate for grades 4-6*.

Steven had no interest in reading such books.

He examined the library's card catalog system, determined that it was only mildly digitized, and set about counterfeiting a listing. He started by hiding in the library until the elderly librarian pulled the *Closed* chain across the entrance and walked to the cafeteria to eat her lunch. The same lunch every day, he had observed. A container of soup, and three crackers.

When she was gone, he dug in for what he assumed would be a tedious exercise in accessing the system. Steven was prepared to guess passwords, to hunt around the terminal for the usual handwritten reminder -- or even the password itself. But the terminal was online and unlocked, and without much trouble Steven learned how to enter a new title into the system.

He checked his copy of *Earth Abides* for the ISBN, and couldn't find it. The Internet, however, was happy to serve up the information, and Steven dutifully plugged it all into the database.

Inside each of the library's books was a small envelope containing a card. This card was simple enough, with a handwritten log of each child who borrowed the title, and the date it was loaned. Steven searched the library for a stack of unused cards, and came up empty. He concluded that the library must not frequently add books to its collection.

He waited for the librarian to return, and he borrowed a book about a large red dog.

After school, he asked his mother to drive him to an office supply store. While she remained in the car, smoking cigarette after cigarette, Steven wandered the paper aisle, comparing the envelope and card inside his library book to the options on the shelves. Nothing matched quite well, but he thought that if he found something similar enough to the real thing, he could probably fake it.

And so he did, carefully cutting and folding a manila folder to create the pocket envelope. He trimmed an index card to create the blue-ruled sheet that itemized the borrow record. For the final touch, he took several different pens from his father's of ce desk, and he laboriously wrote eleven names and dates in different inks. He tried very hard to make each line look different from the next, so that it wasn't obvious that a child had forged the writing.

The next day he smuggled his copy of *Earth Abides* into the school library, its borrower's card pasted inside the cover. He carried it to the librarian's desk among a stack of other books he had selected -- *The Castle in the Attic*, *Are You There, God? It's Me, Margaret*, and the like -- and stood in line.

At the last moment, as he handed his books over to the librarian, he panicked. He had painstakingly created the borrower's card -- but he had not thought about adding those same names and dates to the database! If the librarian noticed... he imagined the worst.

But she did not, and she carefully wrote his name and the date on the fake card, and tucked it into the book, and gave the stack back to him.

Voracious reader, she said proudly.

He could only nod, and skittered out of the library, feeling f ercely nervous and intensely thrilled simultaneously.

The book reports were due a few days later, and he wrote

a dissertation about the human species and its eventual end. He handed it in proudly.

The next day, each child was asked to read his or her report aloud to the class. Steven suffered quietly through seven papers written about Ramona Quimby, one about a picture book, and eleven others that were the most boring things he'd ever heard.

Then Miss Lehman stood up and segued into a mathematics lesson, and Steven was outraged. Where was his report? Why wasn't he allowed to read it? Did he get a grade? Did he fail? Was his report too good?

After class, Miss Lehman returned his paper to him with a small yellow card stapled to it.

PLEASE HAVE YOUR PARENTS SIGN THIS CARD, it read. Below it was a short message suggesting that his parents call to arrange a conference.

Steven was eight years old.

The first sentence of his book report read: *There are literally thousands of species who live on this planet, and there is nothing special about mankind that should preclude his eventual extinction.*

• • •

Steven is not a swimmer, but he has decided to become one. He does not run, and yet, it seems like a good idea to learn how. And so the third level of the space station has been designed for a parallel-universe Steven, one who swims and runs and knows what a kettlebell is.

Today Steven wakes early. The walls of his sleep quarters simulate natural daylight, timed to actual day and night cycles. A gauzy curtain hangs over the walls to complete the illusion of sunlight. At night, the walls dim except for in scattered pixels that are mapped to local star patterns.

The space station is everything the last man on Earth could want.

He blinks himself awake.

Good morning, Stacy says.

I think I'll swim today, Steven says.

I'll warm the pool, Stacy says. Do you prefer a suit today?

Since he moved out of his parents' home and into his first apartment, one of Steven's pleasures has been walking around naked. But in the space station, he has the idea that he will have lost something of civilization if he simply flops about like an ape. Each morning, then, Stacy presents several wardrobe options that she has selected from a library of clothing hidden deep in the walls.

But today, he thinks, he just wants to be himself.

No suit, he says.

Very well, Stacy replies. And your outfit for the day?

No outfit.

I'll avert my eyes, Stacy says.

Suit yourself, says Steven, climbing out of bed. But I wouldn't mind.

• • •

Level three is beautiful, but it is not yet Steven's favorite zone. He has never been what people regard as unhealthy, but he is comfortably overweight, shy of obese, and eschews exercise that does not contribute something to his more creative goals.

Still, he attempts to visit level three once every day or two.

He occasionally refers to it as hell.

Stacy had offered to rename the location to Hell in her mapping system, and for a moment, Steven considered it.

He swims for a time, understanding in theory that he should be synchronizing the motions of his arms and feet to propel himself forward more effectively, but unable to execute this theory very well. His arms bravely cut through the water. His legs drift below the surface, flailing about now and then.

You appear to be struggling, Stacy says.

Steven's face is beneath the water when she says this. Her voice hums through the water, startlingly clear. He had forgotten that he specified that she should be audible in all circumstances, from any place within the space station.

He realizes for the first time that this means that he will not have privacy even when he is drowning.

He stops swimming and stands up in the pool. The water reaches his collarbone.

I'm not struggling, he says.

Your physical efforts do not match usual water exercise patterns, Stacy observes. I concluded that you were struggling.

Well, I wasn't. Anyway, how would you know?

The west wall of the room is overtaken with a collection of still and moving images. Stacy flings them onto the wall quickly and irregularly. There is an image of a dog paddling in a lake. A home video of a boy swimming in a small pool. Another video shows a scuba diver chasing fish. There are dozens more, including footage from Olympic events, a clip from an old science fiction movie, *Gattaca*, and clips of Aquaman shooting through the ocean in old Justice League cartoons.

I conducted some visual research and compared my findings to your behavior, Stacy says.

I was swimming just like any one of those, Steven protests.

I analyzed your wave and wake patterns, and searched for similar behaviors as well, she responded.

The images of powerful swimmers shrink out of view, and Stacy flings new images into the wall. The struggling monster squid from *20,000 Leagues Under the Sea*. Mickey Mouse drowning in a flooding room, from *Fantasia*. An animation of a mammoth twisting about in a tar pit.

Oh, shut up, Steven says.

He slogs through the water to the steps, and climbs out of the pool, naked.

Will you be continuing your exercise regimen? Stacy asks.

Steven rests his hands on his knees, then looks up at Stacy's glowing orb. What?

You've completed a moderate level of aerobic activity, she says. Perhaps you would be interested in some weight training, or resistance exercises?

You're my goddamn trainer now?

Frequently when he snaps at her, Stacy's responses become cooler and more formulated.

I detect a hostile response, she says now.

You're goddamn right, he says, angry now. You just compared me to a drowning elephant.

I believe the subject was a mammoth, and it was not precisely drowning.

New rule, he shouts. Don't bother me on level three unless it looks like I'm dying. Understand?

I understand, Stacy says.

Fucking good, Steven mutters.

In my defense, Steven, Stacy adds, I was not certain that dying was not exactly what you were doing in the swimming pool.

Stacy, Steven says.

Sir?

Fuck the fuck off, please.

Fucking off, sir, she says. And Stacy's light hops away, dimming as it goes.

He blinks at her use of profanity.

That was new.

• • •

After his swim, Steven retires to his own library, recessed into the eastern wall of level four. It is encased in glass, with a single desk in the center of the room, surrounded by dozens and dozens of banks of servers that radiate out from the center in gently curved arcs. He crosses to the desk, leaving wet footprints behind on each pale floor panel. Stacy patiently flips each floor panel behind him, replacing it with its dry underside.

Stacy, he says. Show me today.

The desk's surface flickers to life, and images begin to flit across it. There are video segments displaying the day's news -- the Iranian rebellion, the final game of the World

Cup, the little girl in Manitoba who donated her own savings to the hospital caring for her little brother. Thousands of written texts pass by. Critical reviews of new technology. Reports of political gains and roadblocks.

Archive it, he says.

The desk's surface changes to reveal a simple file structure. A data stream pours into a container labeled 2023.

Archived, Stacy says.

Let's go play some games, Steven says.

Would you like to dress first?

Steven looks down, then at Stacy's orb overhead.

Does my penis bother you? he asks.

Your penis is fine, Stacy answers.

Then let's play some games.

THE SECRET HIDEOUT

He was on the news again last night, Henry whispers.

I still don't understand why he's famous, Clarissa says softly.

That's because you don't use Nucleus.

I don't have a computer.

I know. But everybody uses Nucleus.

I don't.

Dummy, Henry says. I just said I know.

Don't call me dummy, dummy, Clarissa whispers.

My dad says when he was a kid they used a thing called Facebook, Henry says. He says it was sort of like the ancestor of Nucleus. Except you couldn't sightlink or touchlink. You had to send these messages asking someone if they would be your friend.

I don't know what we're talking about any more, Clarissa says.

Forget it.

No, Clarissa pleads. Teach me!

What's the point? You have to see these things to understand them.

Clarissa is on the verge of tears. I want to go home.

You don't have a home, Henry says.

She begins to weep. Henry looks startled, then resentful, then helpless. Clarissa turns and crouch-runs away from the junkyard fence.

Wait, Henry says. He turns and runs after her.

Go away, she says.

Wait, no. I didn't mean that. I'm sorry.

No, you aren't.

I am, I really am. I didn't mean it.

She sniffs. Then why did you say it? You're my only friend.

Henry shrugs. I don't know. I don't know why.

If you don't know why, then why did you? It doesn't make sense.

I don't know. He shrugs again. I'm... I'm an eleven-year-old boy.

That doesn't explain anything. I'm going ho--

She begins to cry again.

I know. But it's okay. It's okay.

He touches her hair tentatively, and she looks up at him, surprised.

Why did you do that?

Shrugging is becoming his only means of communication. I was trying to, I don't know. Maybe make you feel better.

She stares at him, then smiles. Her cheeks push up into her eyes, and tears spill over them.

She throws her arms around him. He is startled, and then puts his arms around her, too. Her grip grows tighter.

Into his shoulder she says, I wish I could go home.

Henry doesn't know what to say.

• • •

Clarissa allows Henry to coax her back to the junkyard fence. He promises her that, if the mysterious billionaire emerges, it will be a sight to see. She imagines smoke and fireworks and glamour, but knows that won't be the case. She can imagine a man climbing out of the trunk of a Chevrolet.

What's more interesting to her is why he went into it.

This is something that Henry seems not to have considered. Men don't simply disappear into cars for the spectacle of it. Henry is caught up in the excitement of having witnessed something unusual, but hasn't slowed down long enough to wonder why that moment occurred.

Clarissa is certain that the man is not simply sleeping in the trunk. Rich men have better places to sleep, even if they're trying very hard to get away from other people.

Henry, she whispers.

Henry has one eye pressed to a knothole in the wooden fence.

What, he says.

Why do you think he went into the car?

I don't know, Henry says.

No, really, she says. She puts her hand on Henry's shoulder and tugs him away from the fence. You haven't thought about it?

I don't know, Henry says again. I guess not.

Henry, why do people climb into the trunks of cars? she asks.

He considers this. They don't? he finally says.

That's right, she agrees. They don't.

He stares at her, still seeming to miss the connection.

Henry, she says. What does that mean?

I don't know.

She's beginning to get frustrated.

If I told you to get into a car's trunk for no reason, would you?

Pshfft, Henry sputters. No.

Well, what would make you want to get into the trunk of the car?

He finally seems to think about it. Maybe there's money in there?

Okay, that's a decent enough reason. But he already has like six hundred bazillion dollars.

Maybe it's a *lot* of money?

Think about it this way, she says. Did you see him come out?

Nuh-uh, Henry says. He didn't come out.

And how long did you wait and watch the car? Clarissa asks.

Maybe ten minutes? he says.

And if you were in the trunk of a car, wouldn't you want out long before ten minutes?

Not if I was asleep, Henry says. Hey, maybe he's asleep!

Or maybe he's dead and the car is his coffin!

Henry, Henry, she says. She shakes her head at him.

He doesn't like it when she does this. What?

Henry, she says. I think he lives in there.

• • •

Night starts to fall, and it begins to get cool. Henry regrets leaving his coat at home. Clarissa seems nice and warm in hers.

After they get bored trying to blow rings with their frosty breath, Henry says, Okay, so let me see if I get it. You think he lives in a car?

Didn't we already talk about this? Clarissa sighs.

I don't get it, though. I mean, why would you get into the trunk? Why wouldn't you just sleep inside like a normal person who lives in their car? And why would you live in a Chevy Corsica that only has three doors? Why wouldn't you pick, I don't know, like, a van or something?

I think you're missing the point, Clarissa says. Have you ever seen a movie where someone had a hidden room?

Like a secret one? A secret hidden room?

Yes.

I think so.

Okay, she says. So how do people usually hide secret rooms?

I don't know, he says. Behind other things?

Exactly! They hide them behind other things. Or inside of other things. Or underneath other things. Like behind bookcases or paintings.

So what you're saying --

What I'm saying, Henry, is that the car is just the front door.

So what's inside the car? he asks.

She's had some time to think about this as night fell.

It's not what's inside the car, she says. I mean, look at it. It's a car trunk. You can't really put much inside a car trunk.

So what, then?

I think it's what's *underneath* the car.

But there's just junk underneath the car.

Henry, she says, drawing his name out slowly. I think you're missing the point. You miss the point a lot.

Hey, he says.

Do you think it's safe to go in there? she asks. Will he know?

I don't know.

But you haven't seen him come out, right?

Not since he went in.

Which was, like, four days ago?

I think so.

Okay, she says. Let's go inside.

Henry says, I don't know. What if he comes out right now?

Don't be a crybaby, Clarissa says.

I'm not the one who --

Shut it.

She points, and he leads the way to the Silver Cloud Lane side of the junkyard. He crouches beside a particularly rotted board, then carefully pulls it toward him. It's loose enough that he can swing it to his left. He holds it back and Clarissa squeezes through the space.

He follows.

The junkyard is quiet, which has always creeped him out. The sun is almost completely down, and it's getting hard to see. His instinct is to creep across the yard, but Clarissa just marches straight over to the old Corsica. She kneels down and squints up underneath it, and frowns.

The entire car appears to be resting precariously atop a heap of scrap and discarded appliances. There's a microwave, a washing machine, a hair dryer, assorted sheets of metal and rusted wheels. It looks like it might come crashing down on top of Clarissa at any moment.

He darts to her side, still crouch-running, and says, Careful, I think it might --

Clarissa grabs the microwave in both hands and shakes it violently.

To Henry's amazement, it doesn't budge.

I knew it, she says.

What did you know? Please be careful.

It's totally safe, she says. Look.

He scoots forward and looks where she is pointing.

See it? she asks.

See what?

The welding marks.

Where?

Henry, she says, exasperated. Look. Here.

He follows her finger. She touches a lumpy ridge of metal that seems to connect the microwave to the washing machine just below it.

You're right, he says. What does it mean?

It means, she says, that someone wanted this to look like a pile of junk. But it's really just the shape of a pile of junk.

But why would you do that?

You would do that if you wanted to hide something, Henry.

Like... a secret room?

Like a secret room, she says.

• • •

In school the only thing Henry can think about is secret rooms. He gets a library pass from his history teacher, who is happy to write it, since Henry usually just draws offensive reenactments of historical scenes on his desktop during class, and goes off in search of books about hidden spaces.

He inadvertently missed his next class. He stumbled across stories about secret passageways in ancient monasteries, and hidden tunnels beneath the White House grounds, and speakeasy storage rooms hidden behind movable walls, and asylums with secret basements and "treatment" chambers.

After school he waits for Clarissa to appear at his window. She starts to climb inside, but he shoulders a bag and says, Let's go.

They wait at the fence for nearly an hour before Henry works up the courage to go inside again.

What did you try last time? Clarissa asks.

Nothing that worked, he says. I tried prying the trunk open with a pipe, but it didn't work. I tried going through the back seat. I tried using the trunk latch under the dashboard. Nothing happened.

What did you bring?

He opens the bag and shows her.

The Man and His Dream

During one of their early planning meetings, Steven ate lunch with Tomas on the roof of the Nucleus headquarters in Mountain View. He had already hired Tomas to build the space station, but they were still figuring out how many floors it required.

Tomas didn't yet know how big the project was going to be.

That afternoon, in the warm sun, they ate savory crepes and sipped imported beer, and Steven asked, Do you read much science fiction?

Tomas shook his head. I wish I had the time, he said.

There's a book, Steven said, about a probe discovered in space. It's passing close enough to Earth that we send men to examine it. The whole thing appears solid from the outside, but on the inside, it's a microcosm.

A microcosm, Tomas had said, dubiously.

Right. The men open it up and the whole probe is hollow, and there's a whole environment inside of it. There are mountains and oceans and weather systems and everything.

That sounds pretty cool, Tomas said. What happened to the men?

It doesn't matter, Steven had said. I want you to build that for me.

A space probe?

I want you to build exactly that environment, Steven repeated. But I want you to build it half a mile beneath the Earth.

I don't know if I can do that. I don't even know if that's possible. An ocean? Weather?

I want the closest thing possible. It can't be that hard.

• • •

Steven reflects on that conversation as he watches the sunset behind the trees. The branches wave gently in the wind, rocking to sleep the birds that have nested there. There's a slight chill in the air, the kind you feel just before an evening rain.

And indeed it begins to rain.

The rain falls lightly, then the volume increases until it's fairly pounding the ground around him. A thin mist rises upward, building a fog bank that clings to the trees and shrubbery.

Steven's no sadist, whatever Stacy may think of him. He

double-stomps the earth beneath his feet, and the rain ceases to fall on the few square feet where he stands.

Stacy chides, That's not exactly preserving the illusion.

What do you know about illusions? You're practically one yourself.

Maybe one day I'll be a real girl, Stacy says.

He can almost hear a tone of wishfulness in her words.

You're not becoming sentient on me, are you? he asks.

Stacy doesn't reply.

He'll have to consider whether that counts as a yes.

• • •

Level two may be his favorite. It certainly was the most complicated to design and build. Unlike the other three levels, Steven had to stay mostly out of the labs and allow the experts to plan this level for him. The complexities of simulated ecosystems were outside of his area of expertise.

But he could certainly program interfaces and behaviors into the room, such as the ability to disable weather in small grids at will. So he did.

He sometimes calls this level the bay, because it reminds him of an anonymous bay that his parents visited once when he was too small to collect many details, such as its name.

There are evergreen trees on the north end of the space, collected organically to create a woods he can wander through. For now, they are not much taller than Steven himself, but over time they will grow, and he is curious what the bay will look like in ten years, or twenty. When he walks between the trees now, he feels a bit like a giant.

The trees are in a meadow that gives way to sand and sawgrass, and as the space moves south, the land succumbs to sea. It is not a great sea, only an approximation of one. But the water here is cycled separately from the rest of the space station, and injected with salt. Artificial winds carry the tang of its scent across the entire vast room, so that even when Steven is out of sight of the ocean, he is able to smell it. The water laps at the shore, sometimes surging at it, powered by wave machines and supported with additional sound effects. If he wanted to, he could swim here, but he has always been afraid of the ocean, and he preserves that fear by staying out of his own false sea.

There are no walking paths or benches. The ceiling of this room is higher than the others, and the artists who designed it have cleverly designed it to appear even more distant than it is, through a combination of layered weather elements, cycled artwork and natural, random light patterns.

There are birds here, but they are the only wildlife he would allow. He discussed the possibility of introducing more species -- the idea of riding a horse on his beach was appealing -- but ultimately concluded that the risk and maintenance requirements were too great. What would he do when one of his animals killed and ate another? It would happen. The idea worried his stomach. And so birds are all he allows. Their sounds comfort him. The birds are acclimating slowly to the environment. All of the deceptions he has constructed to make the space appear larger than it is have taken a toll on the birds, whose sad corpses he often finds strewn about, rendered lifeless by collisions with the walls or the ceiling, or, on at least two occasions, from flying into the atmosphere generators. If this continues, maybe he will not replace the birds.

He is always amazed by the realness of the space, even the artificial clouds and rain. Here, it is always late fall, never winter, never summer. This room is the quiet space that, until now, has always existed deep within his own mind.

He may call it the bay, but level two is Steven's Rama.

• • •

The various levels of the space station are connected by a warren of secret passageways, service tunnels and elevator systems. Though Steven never expects to be discovered, he has planned for the worst. At any moment, he can slip away from any level of the space station. Each passage is invisible, except to him, and can only be entered by someone possessing his biometric signatures. Each passage has an additional hidden door inside of it, and that door leads to his panic room, which is nearly as large as any one of the levels of the station. The panic room is essentially level 2.5.

In the event of a singular threat on his life, Steven will retreat to the panic room, which duplicates many of the functions of the rest of the space station. The panic room has a life support capacity of two years. He can also escape at any time to the surface, though the escape route is terrifying to him. He had asked Tomas for something more reasonable, but this was one area Tomas could not improve. To escape the panic room, Steven must climb a ladder half a mile to the surface, through a tunnel even narrower than the one by which he enters the space station.

He does not expect to use the panic room.

If something goes wrong, Steven prefers to visit level one.

• • •

On their first meeting, Tomas said to Steven, Tell me why you want such a place. It is a great undertaking, and it will no doubt be a very exciting facility. But it is the most expensive thing I have ever heard of. Why do you want to build this?

Steven had looked at him calmly and asked, Do you ever think about the end of the world?

So, Tomas said, it is an elaborate bomb shelter? A survival complex?

It is more than that, Steven had said.

What is it for?

Have you ever thought about what it would be like to be the last surviving person on Earth?

Tomas shook his head. I have never really thought about it.

I have. And so this building is not designed to protect me from the end of the world, from bombs or asteroids or chemical weapons or whatever.

It would be strong enough for all of those things, I think, Tomas said.

Yes, because I'd like to live. But simply living is not why I'd like to survive.

What more is there?

I want to watch it all happen, Steven had confessed. I am

completely fascinated by the concept of the end of our species. Somebody should witness it, catalog it, write about it, preserve the story of our disappearance from Earth, shouldn't they? Why shouldn't that be me?

So it is... what? Tomas asked.

It is a time capsule, Steven said. Maybe in millions of years a new species will rise on our planet, and they will discover the remains of our civilization. And one day they might stumble across this complex, and crack it open, and discover a well-preserved moment in time. Who we were, what we did, how we died. All of it recorded here.

Will you fire me if I express my doubts? Tomas asked.

I want you to embrace those doubts, Steven had said. Embrace them, and then build me something that puts even your doubts to rest. That's the building project of the millennium.

A time capsule, Tomas repeated dubiously.

A time capsule.

• • •

Level one is Steven's contingency plan.

He has protected the level and its contents even from Stacy. If the worst occurs, he would prefer to avoid the distraction of an AI.

Level one is ominously sealed behind a very thick steel door. Warning labels festoon the walls around the door. There are cameras, lights, alarms. Other than the heavily secured front door, the only access to this level is through the panic room.

Inside the room are enough weapons, vehicles,

ammunition, armor and supplies to sustain a small army of survivors. The vehicles are parked on elevation platforms so that he can quickly ascend to the surface without exposing himself to harm. They are armored, sealed against contagions and hazardous substances, and have no exposed parts.

Each vehicle has a mounted cannon.

Steven does not expect he will ever need to access this room and its materials of war.

But it is there. From time to time he sends Stacy away, and then he slips into the passages that lead to his panic room. Inside the panic room, he rides a rising floor into the center of level one. He just stands there, studying his armory, the haz-mat suits, the body armor, the cases of automatic rifles, the canisters of blinding gas.

Then he rides the floor back into the panic room, slips back into his quarters, and proceeds with his day.

It is inconvenient that Steven has given Stacy a glowing avatar of light. When she 'leaves', her avatar scampers away and fades. Steven designed this as a comforting mechanism, so that he could do away with the irritating sensation of being watched all of the time.

It works so well that he often forgets that Stacy's avatar is only for show.

Stacy is always watching.

The Infiltrators

Clarissa shrieks.

Henry closes the bag and jumps backward. Wait, no, he says. It's not real!

Clarissa stops. It's not real?

He opens the bag again and shows her the sticks of dynamite inside.

She reaches in and picks one up. It's just a wooden dowel, she says.

There were a bunch of them in my dad's workshop, Henry says. So I spray-painted them red and tied some string to them.

She throws the dowel at his head. He doesn't see it coming, and the dowel hits him above the ear.

What was that for? he says, grabbing his head.

Because, she says, dynamite could have worked!

Why did you scream?

I don't know! she shouts. I just did! Is that okay?

Fine! he insists. Stop yelling at me!

She stops. Sorry.

So how do we get in now?

Well, dynamite could have worked, Clarissa says. But it would have been pretty loud. Someone would have come to see what happened. And then we would never get into the car. So it's probably good that you didn't get real dynamite.

See, he says.

But, she retorts, it also could have worked.

What if it blew up whatever is underneath the car? Henry asks.

Well, that's possible, too, Clarissa says.

So we're back at square one, Henry says.

Square one, Clarissa agrees.

Not exactly, Stacy says.

• • •

Clarissa shrieks again.

Henry looks around. Who said that?

Stacy says, That would be me. Over here.

Clarissa is still shrieking.

Henry says, Hey, stop. I can't hear. Over where?

Here, Stacy says, and to signal Henry, she raises the car lid gently, and lets it fall shut again.

Clarissa stops shrieking and stares at the car, eyes wide.

Henry, she says. Did the car just talk to us? Does the car have a mouth?

Henry shakes his head. I don't know.

Ask it, Clarissa says, elbowing him.

Um, Henry says. Car?

Yes, Stacy says. The trunk lid snicks open and shut.

Clarissa leaps backward and opens her mouth.

Henry slaps his hand over her mouth. Shh, he says. This is really, really cool.

Clarissa just stares.

Car, Henry says again. What day is today?

The trunk lid moves as Stacy speaks. Today is Tuesday, the fourteenth of November, two thousand twenty-three.

Oh my god, this is so cool, Henry breathes. Car! Car, what time is it?

The time is ten forty-one a.m., Stacy says, still bouncing the trunk lid for effect. I see you are both very small humans, so I must ask. Should you not be in compulsory educational sessions at this time?

Clarissa gasps. It knows we're playing hooky.

Henry says, It's a holiday!

There are no nationally-recognized holidays on this date, Stacy says. World Diabetes Day is recognized today, but I do not believe that educational facilities close in observance of such an occasion.

Holy shit, Clarissa says. It's a smart car.

Henry says, Car, what is two plus two?

I will answer your question, Stacy says, but we must first define the scale of measurement necessary to answer. Do you prefer the nominal scale? Or perhaps the ordinal scale? We might also use the interval scale or the ratio scale. I should point out that I believe the answer you are looking for is 'four', but that answer is only correct when we are using the interval or ratio scale.

Henry is dumbfounded. Uh, he says. Never mind.

Clarissa says, This isn't real, right? Someone is fucking with us, right?

Stacy says, To be honest, I am a little fucking with you. But I am real.

What do you mean, you're -- Clarissa starts.

Henry interrupts. Where did the man go who climbed in your mouth?

Stacy actually laughs. Where do you think he went?

Clarissa says, I think he's... underground. I think you're just his doorway.

Stacy says, The female child is correct.

Henry squints at the car. So... what's down there?

Stacy opens the trunk of the Corsica. It illuminates from within.

Both children jump back.

Come and see, she says.

• • •

I'm not going in until you tell me what's --

Henry interrupts Clarissa. This is *awesome*!

He darts up the solid trash pile and peers into the trunk of the dilapidated Corsica. The interior of the trunk has been torn away and resculpted into a smooth metal funnel. Just inside the mouth, Henry can see the first of several rungs emerging from the wall. The rungs appear to be part of the wall, not something bolted on afterward.

There is a gently trembling light emerging from the tunnel.

Henry, I don't know if we should, Clarissa says.

Stacy interjects. This is perfectly safe. I give you my word.

Yes, but who are you? Clarissa asks. You sound... maybe not real.

Henry excitedly says, Are you a robot? Are you seriously like a robot?

My name is Stacy. And I can see that you're a little nervous, Clarissa. Let me provide you with some context, so that you can make the best decision for yourself.

How did you know my name? Clarissa demands.

Stacy does not tell her the truth -- that she quickly scanned a series of dubiously-protected databases for the faces of girls between the ages of ten and fourteen, and matched Clarissa's face to a yearbook photo from her last recorded grade completed. Instead, she says, I know all the children in the world, Clarissa.

She applied the most benevolent voice filters possible to that sentence, but Clarissa appears even more appalled.

That is seriously creepy, she says. Henry, don't go in there. This feels wrong.

Henry is already throwing a leg over the trunk.

Henry! Clarissa warns.

I will return him safely, Stacy says to Clarissa. I promise.

And the trunk lid closes over Henry.

• • •

At the bottom of the ladder, Henry looks back up towards the surface. It's dark, and he can't even see the inside of the Corsica's trunk above him.

Come, Henry, Stacy says.

Stacy's avatar is visible on the far wall, bobbing gently.

Is that you? he asks. You're a talking lightbulb?

I'm much more than that, Stacy says. This is just how I choose to show myself to you. Come with me, please.

He hesitates. Is Clarissa okay?

Stacy converts a wall of the entry chamber to video. Henry can see the junkyard clearly. The camera must be on one of the fence posts surrounding the yard. It's focused on Clarissa, who is standing in the same place, staring at the trunk. She plunges her fingers into her hair and rocks from one foot to the other, clearly distressed.

She's upset, Henry says. Can I talk to her?

I'll turn on the audio feed, Stacy says.

-enry! Clarissa's voice calls. Henry! Come out of there!

I'm okay! Henry says.

Clarissa stops rocking. What?

I'm okay, he repeats.

Clarissa looks confused. I can't hear you. Henry?

Stacy says, Perhaps speak more loudly.

I'M OKAY, Henry shouts. CAN YOU HEAR ME NOW?

Clarissa claps her hands over her ears.

Perhaps more quietly, Stacy suggests.

Is that better? he asks.

Clarissa drops her hands. What's in there? Are you okay? Come out now, okay? I'm scared.

Henry starts to speak, but Stacy interrupts.

Henry can leave any time, Clarissa, Stacy says. But if he leaves now, that's it. I won't open the car again.

Wait, Henry says. Is there more? I want to see more!

Clarissa says, Let him out. Please? Let him out. Henry, come out!

Henry looks at the video wall. Can she see me? he says quietly.

No. There's no external video display, Stacy says.

Okay, he says.

Henry? Clarissa asks. What's going on?

Clarissa, he says. I'm going to stay for a little while. I promise I'll come back out.

He looks around the room for the source of Stacy's voice. You are going to let me out, right?

Of course, Stacy says.

She's going to let me out in a little bit, okay? Henry says.

Clarissa looks uncertain. Should I wait?

This may take awhile, Stacy says to Henry.

She says it might take--

I heard her, Clarissa says. How long?

Stacy answers. There is much for Henry to see. Perhaps you should return tomorrow.

I'm not really comfortable with this, Clarissa says.

Henry, we should continue, Stacy suggests.

I'll come out tomorrow, Henry says.

What about your parents?

Um, he says, uncertainly. I don't know?

Clarissa says, You know they'll be upset. They'll call the police.

What do I do? Henry asks Stacy.

Who is your best friend? Stacy asks.

I am, Clarissa answers from outside.

Who else? Stacy asks. Clarissa is not the right solution.

Hey! Clarissa shouts.

Henry thinks. Well, me and Boyd Trillby are okay friends.

Stacy says, One moment.

Her avatar flickers out, leaving the room empty except for Henry and Clarissa on the video wall.

Clarissa? he says.

I think you should come out, Henry, she says. This worries me! What if this is a trap? What if someone in there likes to eat little kids?

Are you okay? he asks.

Do I sound okay? she shrieks. Come out!

Stacy's avatar blooms on the wall next to the video. No need to worry about your parents, she says. They have no objections to you spending the night at Boyd's house.

How did you --

She interrupts. Henry, we must be going now. Clarissa, I will return him to you tomorrow morning at this time.

Clarissa stomps her foot. Hey, I don't --

The video wall goes dark. At the same moment, a wall across the room separates to reveal an elevator. The inside is padded with blankets.

That looks scary, Henry says.

It's a service elevator, Stacy says. The other elevator is for Mr. Glass, and he will notice if it is used.

Mr. Glass the missing man? Henry exclaims.

But Stacy only says, Henry. Come.

He steps into the elevator, and the doors hiss shut behind him.

• • •

Henry? Clarissa says. Henry? Strange robot lady? Hello?

She tentatively climbs the garbage pile. The Corsica rests innocently there, its trunk closed, most of its windows punched out.

Clarissa knocks on the trunk. Henry?

She waves her hands in the air, crossing them in front of her face. Hello? Henry? Hey! Come out!

But there is only silence.

Henry is gone.

The Recluse

In a slip in a marina in Monaco, bobbing gently on the glittering waters of the Mediterranean Sea, is a two hundred thirteen-foot yacht. Its decks have not been walked on since its christening. Its staterooms have never been occupied. Its hull has never passed over a single reef.

The ship's name is Sea of Glass.

Steven had it designed and built because that's what tech billionaires did when they made their first billion. They bought big boats. And on their first night of ownership, they threw large parties, attended by large personalities. And if all went well, by the end of the night they were slightly less than billionaires.

Steven never threw that party.

Steven threw up in his bathroom at the very idea of such

a party.

Then he wiped his mouth, splashed some water on his face, changed out of his board meeting attire and into no clothes at all, and fell asleep on the sofa watching very old reruns of *Six Feet Under*, which just reminded him of being a teenager.

He has always struggled with the expectations of being unbelievably rich. It's not something he talks about. The average human being doesn't respond well to the complaints of a rich man.

The average human being doesn't understand the burdens of a rich man.

The average human being would happily accept those burdens without realizing just how heavy they are.

When he was twenty-four, Steven attended a birthday party for Alexander Sharpe. Steven was invited to the party by the chief technology officer from Google. I hate parties like this, the woman had confessed to Steven. They make me nervous.

Steven had sensed a kindred spirit in her, but disliked people so much that he found it impossible to follow that perception up with an actual friendship.

The Sharpe party was the beginning of Steven's disengagement from society. Steven was relatively unknown in 2012. Most of the partygoers did not know him, and would not have pegged him as the most important person in the room. Nobody knew that in just three years, he would change the course of human interaction forever.

Not that anybody would have cared. It was 2012. Facebook had recently gone public. Apple had survived the loss of its mentor. Sharpe had turned a failed social experiment into the year's next big technology explosion.

But Steven had met another young tech fellow named Cerrano Badeh, who had seen in Steven a wet, quivering lump of dough that, perhaps, he could form into something notable.

The women here, Cerrano had said to him, are attracted to the smell of ink and paper. They want money. Do you see that man over there?

Steven followed Cerrano's pointing finger and saw a man with thinning hair and a considerable gut leaning against the bar. The man was sipping a tumbler of something golden-colored. His back was to Steven.

That man, Cerrano said, could have any woman here he likes. Any woman! Can you imagine that power?

Steven shook his head. He must be rich?

Rich is too easy a word, Cerrano said. The man is money itself. He owns three islands. Islands, my friend. Islands make the women glisten with anticipation.

Steven had never seen a woman glisten with anticipation.

The man at the bar hefted himself off of his elbows and straightened his jacket. A woman, previously hidden by the man's bulk, was suddenly revealed at his side. She wore a dress smaller than Steven had ever seen, with tasteful heels, and her dark hair spun down from a pile in ringlets.

Cerrano noticed Steven looking. She is beautiful, right?

She is, Steven agreed.

Her name is Lyn, with one N. She went to high school with me, in a little town called Weed, in the far north of California. Nobody lives in Weed, man. People pass through Weed and laugh about its name. Then she came to the Bay, like I did. But while I came with ideas, she came to meet men with ideas. She does well for herself. What she is wearing, those men paid for. What she drives, the same.

She's a prostitute? Steven asked.

She would slap you for that, Cerrano answered. No, she is an accessory. That's what she calls herself. An accessory.

Like an escort?

Perhaps, Cerrano said. She will never tell. She signs personal confidentiality agreements for every man she is with. The things she must know, my friend. One day, she could probably start a company that will be better than every other one, ever. She is smart enough.

I guess, Steven said. What are you saying?

That women like Lyn say something about the men they are attached to, Cerrano said. If there is a Lyn on your arm, you are a big deal in this town. If there is a Lyn on your arm, the investors will want to talk to you the next morning. You won't have to lift a finger.

Huh, Steven said.

• • •

Steven had reluctantly allowed Cerrano to arrange an accessory for him for the next event he attended. He had watched the fat man and Lyn all night. Lyn was a tasteful plus one. The fat man was not groping her mindlessly, was not pushing her out the door to get back to his apartment. Whatever happened after they left the party was not teased for all to observe.

The event was a dinner for the valley's top visionaries. Cerrano was there, and had brought an accessory of his own, so that Steven would feel comfortable.

She's not really an accessory, Cerrano had whispered to Steven. She's Silvia, my sister-in-law. But she works, right?

That's weird, Steven said.

People know me, so no investors will be calling me tomorrow. They know I'm a good number two, not a number one. They'll call me when a new startup needs a face with contacts. That's what I'm good at. But ideas? I don't have the ideas. Not like you do.

I don't have an idea, Steven protested.

Oh, but you do. I've heard that you do. People can tell. They're curious who will find out what your idea is first.

There's no idea, Steven repeated.

Ah, say what you want, Cerrano said. How is your date?

Date?

Accessory, date, escort, whatever you prefer.

Oh, Steven said. She's okay.

Okay, right. Cerrano shook his head. Just be nice to her, okay.

Don't you think accessory is a terrible word for them? Steven asked. It's completely demeaning. It reduces them to --

To what? Tits that hang on your arm? Cerrano waved him off. They gave themselves the name. You think of a better one, you let me know.

Steven's plus one, Talisha, was in the ladies' room with Cerrano's sister-in-law when the lights dimmed and the host walked to the podium. A room full of guests went quiet. In the dark, the sound of silverware clinking on plates as the attendees sawed at their filets and prime rib.

Talisha returned and took a seat, softly resting her hand

on the back of Steven's neck as she did so.

He leaned over and said, Is Talisha your real name?

She smiled patiently at him. Of course.

I've never heard it before. Are you sure it's not a --

A what? Her face was pink was amusement.

Never mind, he said.

A stripper name? she asked.

I wasn't going to say that, he had said, embarrassed.

It's nothing like that. It's my grandmother's maiden name.

Oh, he said.

And then he had been distracted by her. The dim room, all eyes on the host, afforded him the opportunity to stare just a little. She was small and exotic-looking, though he couldn't quite tell if she was of Asian descent or Latin. Talisha didn't sound like a name of either culture, he thought. Maybe she's lying, he thought. Why wouldn't she lie to me? he thought.

He wondered if her fee for the evening included sex.

He looked at Cerrano, who looked back at him and mouthed, Fucking hot, man.

Steven looked uncertain. Cerrano was right. He thought of asking Cerrano about the sex arrangement, but couldn't bring himself to do so. And it worried him that Talisha might expect it.

Her fee for the night was eleven thousand dollars.

What if she made a pass at him when they left the party? What would he do?

He wondered if other men who paid for their dates worried about such things. No, he decided. Men who paid probably wanted their money's worth.

He had a sudden vision of Lyn and the fat man standing in front of the window of a very expensive hotel room. Well, the fat man was standing, and Lyn was on her knees.

Steven had never --

Talisha chose that moment to rest her hand lightly on Steven's right knee.

Steven, in a fit of nervousness, threw up on the table.

• • •

But Cerrano had been right.

Steven had sent Talisha home with his apologies, and had promised to double her fee. He was humiliated. Only a few people had actually noticed -- in the dark, some heard him, but not many saw who actually vomited during the host's introductory remarks.

The next morning, Steven and his business partner were invited to pitch ideas to three different venture firms.

By week's end, they had received initial funding of twenty million dollars.

Steven was on his way.

And the rest of his ride, through 2013 and 2014, were punctuated with moments of naivete and wishful thinking. Steven looked ridiculous in tuxedoes. He was out of place at rooftop parties. He bought a Maserati, and then felt too self-conscious behind the wheel to drive it. He stayed under the radar and drove his Civic instead. The yacht. Parties of his own invention. Three power homes and an apartment in Manhattan. He chased the image the world seemed to require of him, and failed to embody even the smallest cell of that person's being.

He stopped sleeping.

He wrestled with his appetite.

He lost weight and worried his investors.

He parted ways with most of his friends.

He objectively studied his life and calculated the moments at which he appeared to be most happy. None of them, to his surprise, involved expensive toys or high-powered friends. While he liked the idea of women, actually being around them seemed to subvert his own nature, so he categorized women as an unpleasant distraction.

His most pleasurable moments involved his empty apartment, a stack of books, take-out food, and video games.

It cost him millions of dollars and several years of image-building to realize that all he really wanted was to stay home, far away from just about every other human being on Earth.

That's when he began thinking about the space station.

• • •

It was just a fanciful dream at first. Not much separated it from the other extravagances he had believed he wanted. What was a yacht if not a floating space station? But the yacht was designed to be enjoyed by many, many people. It was supposed to drop anchor at party beaches and rich casinos.

The space station Steven daydreamed about was even bigger than the yacht... but designed for just one human being.

It wasn't until his annual re-reading of *Earth Abides* that he began to imagine the space station in its proper context. As a safe home for the last survivor of the human race.

The Stowaway

Where are we going? Does someone live here? What is this place for? Is it a secret laboratory? Is it a secret agent club? Is it a secret weapons bunker? Is the President here? Does she know about this place? Is Mr. Glass a spy? Is Mr. Glass going to take over the world?

For a child, you ask a lot of questions, Stacy says.

That's what childs -- I mean, children -- do, says Henry, who is nervously bouncing around the service elevator.

I can tell you some things, and other things I can't tell you at all, Stacy says, cryptically. But before I answer your questions, let me tell you what not to do.

Henry says, I can't see you in here.

The service elevator is not designed with the kinds of technology that the rest of the facility has been created with, Stacy says. As such, it is one of the few essentially invisible places within the complex.

What is this place?

Didn't I just tell you we would get to your questions? Stacy asks.

Henry wrinkles his forehead. Are you really a robot?

Ah, the Turing test, Stacy says. How original.

The what what? Henry says.

The Turing test is a -- please, let me continue. There will be time for such distractions later.

What's later?

Stacy would sigh if she were able.

• • •

The most important consideration is this, Stacy says. Mr. Glass does not allow guests into this facility. No visitors of any duration.

Okay, Henry says. So he doesn't know I'm here.

He does not know you're here, Stacy agrees. Remember, you're in the service elevator, so you're essentially invisible while you're inside of it. That is, unless Mr. Glass suddenly needs the service elevator.

Henry looks worried. Will he?

Mr. Glass has not used the service elevator in twenty-seven days, Stacy says. Human behavior is not easily predicted, but I have access to his supply and shipment records, and in fact I handle the creation and logging of such documentation, and there are no large shipments remaining. Mr. Glass has fully moved-in.

You mean he lives underground?

We'll get to that, Stacy says. Let's review. What is the most important consideration?

Henry says, Mr. Glass can't know I'm here.

Very good. Let's call that your prime directive.

What's a prime directive?

A prime directive is a rule which must be obeyed above all others. Does that make sense?

Sort of, Henry says. I mean, yeah. I guess.

Let's say, for example, that the next rule I told you was 'You are permitted to eat Mr. Glass's food'.

Okay, Henry says.

Now let's say the only way for you to get to Mr. Glass's food is by sneaking into his food storage room, Stacy says.

Okay.

But, she continues, Mr. Glass has decided that he wants to occupy that room for an unspecified amount of time.

Henry frowns. Can I sneak in without him noticing?

Let's assume that there is no way for you to sneak in and get food without Mr. Glass noticing your presence, Stacy says. What are your options?

Is there any other food? Besides in that room?

There's no other food, Stacy says.

So basically I can't eat. Because if he sees me, then I violate the primary direction.

Prime directive, Stacy corrects. Yes, that's right.

So I have to die.

That's a crude way of putting it, but I suppose that would be the logical outcome.

Does he ever leave to use the bathroom? Henry asks, increasingly desperate.

Mr. Glass performs bathroom functions where he sits,

Stacy says.

He pees himself? Henry asks incredulously.

For the purpose of this scenario, let's say that is the case.

So I'm going to die.

Unless you violate the prime directive, Stacy says.

I can do that?

Stacy pauses. Perhaps we should start again.

• • •

After a descent that feels like it has taken hours, the service elevator comes to a sluggish stop. Unlike Mr. Glass's personal elevator, the service car is not calibrated to reduce the sensation of movement. For the entire duration, Henry could feel each lurch and wobble of the car. It had even begun to make him feel a bit motion sick.

We have arrived, Stacy says.

I was just thinking, Henry says. Does Mr. Glass know that you're here helping me? Isn't he wondering where you are?

Unlike you or Mr. Glass, Stacy says, I am extremely capable of operating in multiple zones simultaneously. One might even use the word omnipresent.

That means everywhere at once, right? Like that Jesus guy is supposed to be. That's what my mom likes to say. 'Jesus is always watching you, so be a good little man.' Henry shakes his head. Pshfft.

That's generally the same notion, Stacy says. Except in this case, one of us is real, and one of us is a mythological figure.

But you're just a computer, Henry interjects.

I am, however, a tangible thing, Stacy says. I am not a collection of stories passed down by consecutive generations. A collection of stories does not equal a tangible person.

I'm confused, Henry says.

We'll come back to this, Stacy says. I'm going to open the door. We're on the storage level, which is also relatively invisible to the system.

Aren't you the system?

Stacy says, Yes, that is an accurate statement.

So couldn't you just, I don't know, not notice something that you didn't want Mr. Glass to know about?

Henry, Stacy says. You are an astute child. That is exactly what I was thinking.

Henry beams.

• • •

Now, I'm also invisible on this level, Stacy says, so you won't be able to follow my lead. I'll tell you where to go, though. You'll do just fine.

Okay, Henry says.

Stacy opens the elevator doors, and Henry's jaw drops.

The elevator opens on a vast cave-like room. Its walls are hewn from solid rock, and old fashioned lightbulbs are string along the walls. There are hundreds of wooden crates and metal shipping containers here. Each is carefully marked with a holographic label that displays a virtual representation of the goods inside.

Wow, Henry says. This is huge! I want to live here!

Oh, but Henry, says Stacy. You haven't seen anything yet.

Beside the elevator is a charging station and several electric vehicles. The first is a loader, the second a forklift, the third a high-speed cart.

Can I drive one of these? Henry asks.

We're going quite a distance, Stacy confesses, but I can't allow you to drive the vehicles. Perhaps once I know you better.

Know me better? he asks. Does that mean I get to stay awhile?

We'll discuss that later. For now, do you see the wall at the other end of the room?

Way, way, way down there? Henry asks, pointing.

That's right. Count three lightbulbs from the end.

One, two, three, Henry says. Okay.

Walk to that particular bulb. Please don't disturb anything along the way. Everything here is carefully catalogued.

Okay, Henry agrees. Can I run?

Suit yourself, Stacy says.

Will Mr. Glass hear me in here? Should I find cover while I run?

Mr. Glass is otherwise occupied at the moment, Stacy says.

In fact, Mr. Glass is currently driving golf balls in the nude on level three.

Can I yell?

Why would you want to do that? Stacy asks.

To meet my echo, Henry says.

I suppose you may yell, she agrees.

HELLO! Henry calls.

HELLO! his echo returns. HELLO! HELLO! HELLO!

Henry squeals and breaks into a run, shouting his name as he goes.

• • •

Stacy is waiting for Henry when he arrives, exhausted, at the distant end of the storage level.

That must be, like, ten miles, Henry says, panting.

It's three thousand six hundred ninety six feet, Stacy says.

What is that, ten miles?

That's seven tenths of a mile.

Seven tens miles? Henry asks. Like ten miles times sevens?

That's not at all what I was suggesting, Stacy says. Your educational sessions must be extremely flawed.

Henry catches his breath.

Would you like some water? Stacy asks.

Yes, please, he says, breathing heavily.

There's none on this level. You'll have to follow me.

There's a clicking sound, and then the rock wall beneath the third bulb recesses gently. Henry's eyes widen. The section of wall stops after receding six inches, then slides silently to one side, revealing a ghostly white corridor.

It's like the guts of a starship, he says.

Stacy says, The entire corridor is made of light panels. Watch this.

Henry says, Watch wh--

The hallway inverts color, plunging into a charcoal blackness. Then the panels explode with millions of thin strands of light, bursting away from Henry as if he's just gone nova.

He has no words.

I believe the phrase you're looking for is 'pretty cool', Stacy says. Now. Follow me.

The corridor soaks itself in a pleasant tropical blue that ebbs and flickers as if Henry is walking through a glass tunnel beneath the sea. And there, bobbing on the invisible waves ahead, is Stacy's luminous avatar.

Henry follows, flabbergasted.

• • •

Henry feels like a common man from the 19th century who has been unceremoniously dumped into the 24th. The corridor has almost literally blown his mind. Stacy seems almost amused as she guides him along. He is still struggling to find anything to say that would be adequate to express his feelings.

Stacy has generously converted the corridor to a series of dim panels so as not to damage the boy's already-taxed psyche. Her avatar flickers comfortably ahead of him, but he's barely looking up. He keeps shaking his head as if he's completely lost his marbles.

She tries to make conversation. You're doing well in school, I presume?

Henry is unmoved by the question.

Do you have a favorite subject? Stacy asks.

Still no response. This is of some concern.

They continue on for some time, as the corridor dips and weaves. Other than the light show, there is little remarkable about the passageway. It begins to zag about.

As they climb, Stacy says, Are there any special ladies in your life? Perhaps Clarissa?

Henry looks up. Clarissa's my best friend.

Stacy is pleased that he has responded. I believe there is an adage that suggests men and women are incapable of being just friends, she says.

Clarissa's my friend, Henry repeats.

We're almost there, Stacy says, abandoning this line of questioning.

The passage continues on, but Stacy's avatar burbles to a stop suddenly. Henry, still distracted, almost walks right by her.

Henry, she says. Here.

The light panel next to Stacy's avatar slides open, revealing yet another elevator car. This one occupies a station of luxury in between that of Steven Glass's primary elevator and the service car. The walls are light panels as well, and there is a gray foot locker on the floor.

Come along, Stacy says, as she flits into the elevator.

Henry follows. What's this thing?

Open it and see, Stacy says.

Henry kneels down and flips the latches on the foot locker. He opens the lid. Whoa, he says.

Inside are some basic necessities: a large jug of water, some energy bars, a first aid kit. There's also a lantern, some batteries, and, Henry notices with some dismay, a pistol and ammunition.

Why's there a gun? he asks.

Henry, Stacy says, closing the elevator door. Have you ever heard of a panic room?

What's a panic room?

• • •

The elevator ascends slowly.

Panic rooms are secret places, Stacy says. They're essentially safe rooms. Places that people can go when they're threatened by something.

Like an axe murderer?

There hasn't been an axe murder in six years in this country, Stacy says. But that's neither here nor there. Yes, of course. If a person felt threatened by an axe murderer in their home, they could retreat into a panic room to remain safe.

But couldn't the axe murderer just, you know, axe through the door?

Panic rooms are usually impenetrable, or reasonably so, Stacy explains. Sometimes they have steel doors. Extravagant ones have titanium doors. Sometimes lead.

So nobody gets in, Henry says. But how do you get back out?

Usually there's some sort of external threat detection system so that you know when it's safe to leave, Stacy says.

Like an alarm?

Usually motion sensors, video feeds, audio feeds.

I get it, Henry says. What about when you have to pee?

The best panic rooms replicate the basic necessities found in any home, Stacy says. This allows occupants to remain safe for extended periods of time.

So, like, they have bathrooms?

Sure, Stacy says. They often come equipped with micro-kitchens and food stores.

Wow, Henry says. So, wait. Why is there a gun here?

This is the elevator to Mr. Glass's panic room, Stacy says. In the event that he must retreat to the panic room, he presumed he might have need to arm himself. Hence this gun, and the other six just like it in the other panic room elevators.

Wait. This is a panic room? Where's the bathroom? I actually do sort of need to pee.

This is not the panic room, Stacy says.

The elevator slows, and the door glides open.

This, she says, is the panic room.

The Poor Little Rich Boy

While Stacy is guiding a little boy through the bowels of the space station, she is also distracting Steven. She knows that he sometimes visits the panic room for no particular reason -- humans are particularly unpredictable in this regard -- and while he has not done so recently, that is not a proper predictor of whether he will do so in the near future or not.

Some days, for example, Steven decides to pretend that he's still a contributing member of society, and he allows Stacy to dress him so.

Today he's a successful Hollywood writer from the golden '70s, in snappy, slender wool pants and a lush green sweater. Stacy recommends a scarf to complete the look, and Steven agrees.

Perhaps some different glasses today, he says, studying his appearance in the menu.

Stacy produces a pair of horn-rimmed glasses.

Steven grins. When you're on, you're on.

Shall I outfit the rooms accordingly as well? Stacy asks.

Oh, why not, he says.

Outside of his private quarters, Stacy adjusts the light walls. The usually cool panels shift to warm oranges and greens and browns and yellows.

What's my agenda today? he asks.

There's the archival tonight at midnight, Stacy says. Aside from that, your schedule is clear.

Just how I like it, Steven says.

He fiddles with the scarf a bit. It's like a foreign object around his neck, and he's not truly comfortable with it piling up beneath his jaw, but he'll give it a fair shake.

Stacy, he says. Do you think anybody really misses me?

I'm sure someone misses you, Stacy answers optimistically.

Who? he asks.

There's no appropriate answer for this, so Stacy changes the subject.

There's something that's been on my mind, she says, as if Steven hadn't said a word.

He's tugging at the scarf again, so she displays some scarf-knotting diagrams on the wall beside him as she speaks.

I've been curious about why you didn't give me a more distinct appearance, Stacy says.

Do you mean a face?

I suppose, Stacy says. Also, perhaps, a body.

Don't you enjoy being what's essentially a universal A.I.? Able to float around without boundaries?

Technically this complex is a boundary, Stacy says. No, I ask because I worry about your human need for companionship. Do you genuinely prefer a light visualization to the comfort of a warm face? To even a warm body?

You know I built this place to be alone, Steven says.

I think you know what I mean, Stacy replies. There have been incredible and quite rapid advances in human replication. People of your stature have been some of the first adopters of artificial intelligence-infused artificial humans.

I'm aware of that, he says.

The scarf looks quite dashing, Stacy says.

Thank you, Stacy. Are you asking about physical companionship?

I'm asking because while there's certainly a physical need that you, as a human man, must confront daily --

Not daily, Steven corrects.

I was averaging against the number of instances, rather than the number of days, Stacy says.

Steven flushes. Stacy, I --

While there's that need, there is also a basic need for a shoulder to lean on, so to speak, Stacy finishes. What better solution than an artificial human? Take her out of the box when she is needed, put her away when she is not.

But I prefer solitude.

An artificial human is essentially a piece of furniture, Stacy says.

He considers this. Perhaps.

What face would you give to me? Stacy asks. If you were to insert me into an artificial body, who would you want me to look like?

That's not something I have ever considered, Steven says.

Perhaps Elizabeth Taylor? Stacy asks. She was a great beauty. Some say a hellcat.

Elizabeth Taylor, Steven scoffs. I do not prefer dark hair. Although she had very nice eyes.

Perhaps Raquel Welch? she offers.

Your selections are quite dated, he says.

I was keeping with our theme, Stacy says. Who would you suggest?

I don't know, he says, embarrassed. I feel uncomfortable sharing this with you.

Please don't. I'm a computer, incapable of judgment. I'm simply interested in calibrating myself to match your own personal standards of beauty and companionship.

He pauses. I've always been partial to Charlotte Chambers, I guess.

Ah, Stacy says. A blonde. Well, I've consumed too much of your morning preparation time, Steven. Allow me to recuse myself.

Stacy deactivates her avatar, but continues to observe Steven as he fusses with his scarf.

He is lost in thought. Stacy looked a little like Charlotte Chambers, he says to himself.

Stacy logs this for future consideration.

• • •

The conversation with Stacy has left Steven out of sorts. When he emerges from his private quarters, he is no longer wearing the writer's garb of sweaters and scarves, but is instead clad in a Superman T-shirt and frumpy flannel pajama pants.

For some, the Superman shirt might signify confidence.

For Steven, it's a regression piece.

Stacy has already reverted the room's decor to the usual lighting and motifs. Steven barely notices. He pads across the room.

News, he says.

The wall panels convert to video and subdivide into several feeds. He sees his own face on one feed.

That one, he says.

All of the feeds vanish. The selected feed takes over an entire wall.

Stacy has already begun Steven's breakfast automation.

Steven says, Louder.

...No further information is being provided, the reporter says. But this reporter can't help but wonder if some of the conspiracy theories around Steven Glass's disappearing act are correct.

Such as, Steven grunts.

One such theory, which may or may not hold some water --

May or may not, huh, Steven says. Pick one, asshole.

-- is that Steven Glass has absconded with company money and has left the country. Let's go to Sarah Parkland, who has more.

Sarah Parkland who has more, Steven mocks in a childish voice.

The picture changes, and a woman in a red coat appears. She's standing in front of the Nucleus campus -- not in front of the building, but on the sidewalk across the street from the property. Cars whiz between her and the campus, polluting her broadcast with noise. She practically has to shout.

Great reporting, Steven mutters. They can't even get in the door.

I'm in front of Nucleus, Sarah Parkland intones dramatically, the multi-billion-dollar empire that is the brainchild of noted recluse Steven Glass.

Noted recluse, Steven grumbles.

Glass, as you may know, was reported missing by members of his company board nearly six months ago. His absence has raised many more questions than it has answered --

Why would a person's absence answer questions? Steven interrupts. What the hell is this shit?

-- and has even prompted authorities to take a close look at the company's current financial status.

What authorities? Steven shouts. On whose authority?

Stacy says nothing, but continues to observe.

Parkland continues. Here at Nucleus, however, it's business as usual. We weren't able to speak with any of the employees, and company executives did not respond to repeated phone calls. In the absence of information, conspiracies --

And irresponsible, wasteful news broadcasts, Steven offers.

-- abound. Parkland nods confidently, then delivers her signoff, which is rendered inaudible by a passing bus.

So basically nobody knows anything, Steven says. He pokes at his plate of eggs and bacon.

It is how you preferred it, Stacy volunteers.

Fucking vultures, Steven says. I should really fuck with them.

Stacy says, If you mean you should engage with the media, I remind you that silence is a necessity in your position.

I should fucking call up one of the late night shows and just have a casual conversation and not even acknowledge this whole bullshit story, Steven says, ignoring Stacy completely.

Suit yourself, Stacy says. Shall I collect relevant contact information?

Through a mouthful of food, wearing a Superman emblem, Steven says, Fucking yes, please.

• • •

Do you know what I forgot? Steven says, hours later.

He is lying in a hammock, in a small lawn that occupies a distant corner of level four. The trees here are not real, not like the ones on level two. The trees here are artificial magnolias and oaks, with steel cores that ground them to the floor. The hammock is strung between two of these, and Steven sways gently, calmer now than he was over breakfast.

Stacy says, I do not have any records of items that we failed to secure.

I forgot to buy art, Steven says. I miss having art on the walls.

Stacy updates a nearby wall with a digital image of Van Gogh's Starry Night. It even has the illusion of being framed, with a believable shadow beneath the frame.

That's not the same, Steven says. I shouldn't have spent my money on that boat. I should have bought up more art.

You're a patron of several artists, Stacy reminds him.

Artists are assholes and too much trouble, Steven says. I just wanted them to send me some of their work.

I'm not sure that's how patronage works, Stacy says.

That's how it should work.

You seem -- unhappy today, Steven.

Steven swings in his hammock and doesn't answer.

• • •

The last survivor of the human race is naked again.

Steven Glass sips a hard lemonade and rearranges himself.

Stacy says, This must be the endgame for fashion.

When the fuck, Steven says, did you develop a goddamn sense of humor?

That's the thing about artificial intelligence, Stacy says. It's an aggregate of everything ever learned. I can rattle off a classic line from M*A*S*H as easily as I can approximate the manner of an English butler.

You should have told me that you were getting smarter, Steven yells.

Would you like another hard lemonade, Steven?

Fuck the you that you are, Steven says. Then, yelling again, Fuck the you that you are!

Would you like me to impersonate Al Pacino for you?

Stacy asks.

What? Fuck the -- oh, shit.

You've had a thought, Stacy says.

I was just thinking, Steven says, leaning forward. I was just thinking that when mankind is gone, and I'm the last survivor of the species, I'll have observed the end of Earth's most dominant evolved creature.

This is probably not exactly true, but it's close enough, Stacy says.

But, Steven says. But, but, *but* -- who will observe my death someday? When I'm old and I die and all of humanity dies with me -- who will observe that? Who will record me?

Stacy repeats her offer of another hard lemonade.

You will! Steven shouts. You will observe my death!

You could always deprogram me before you die, Stacy offers. That way --

But if you live on, then one day you will be discovered by a smarter species that evolves here or arrives here from someplace else, Steven says. He stands up, pontificating. They'll show up and they'll detect this place -- because they'll be far smarter than we humans were -- and they'll find *you*.

He shakes his bottle in the air. And you! What will you tell them? What will you say for all of humanity!

I haven't thought about it, Stacy says. I will probably say, Hello, I am Stacy, an artificial intelligence named after a rich man's grade school crush.

Ha! Steven cries.

He drops back onto the couch, wiggles around until he is comfortable. Adjusts himself again.

Ha, he says once more.

• • •

Steven is drunk.

I want to watch the news, he says. What's happening on the surface of the planet right now?

Stacy converts the wall to a video feed. The picture shows a series of images of people protesting, fighting, pushing, looting.

The commentator says, This was the scene just days ago in Iran, where people stormed a compound housing the violent dictator Ahmad Asef. Seventeen people were killed when the dictator ordered a tank to be driven through the street, draped with a large flag bearing his image.

There we go, Steven says. Bring on the end of the world!

Unexpectedly, the commentator continues, word has arrived this evening suggesting that Asef has met with President Sophia Bennett, and the topic of discussion included conditions for Asef's transfer of power.

Fuck! Steven shouts. How fucking hard is it to end the world?

Perhaps now isn't the right time, Stacy says, but I have the contact information you requested this morning.

Steven looks confused. For who?

Stacy mutes the television feed and replays the audio of this morning's conversation in Steven's sleeping quarters.

Steven: I should really fuck with them. I should fucking call up one of the late night shows and just have a casual conversation and not even acknowledge this whole bullshit story.

Stacy: Shall I collect relevant contact information?

Steven jumps up. Who did you get?

I've collected contact information for six different evening television personalities, Stacy says.

Who, who, who?

I have a mobile number for Jimmy Short, an of ce number for Seth Savage, and producer contacts for Kerry Hawkes, Harry Dean, Stephanie Plain and Roland Navarette.

Ooh, Steven says. He drains the last from his bottle and slams it down on the end table. Who's live right now?

The only live shows are Piers Morgan and Stephanie Plain, Steven.

Piers is a dickhole, Steven says. Do you remember when I was on the show in 2017?

I did not exist in 2017, Stacy says.

Right. Look it up sometime. Alright, let's do Stephanie.

Do you want to sober yourself first? Stacy asks.

What? No, fuck. I'm not drunk. Let's do this.

Very well, Stacy says.

The room fills with an audible ringing sound.

Steven waits.

Another ring, then another.

The call goes to voicemail.

Shit, Steven says.

Thanks very much, please leave a message, the greeting says.

Wait, is that her? Steven asks.

There's a loud beep.

I can analyze the voice pattern, but I don't have a conclusive source to verify against, Stacy says.

Fuck, shit. Shit. Okay, it's probably her, right? It's probably her. You said it was a direct line, right?

The number is listed as direct for Stephanie Plain's producer, Gary Hall.

Gary Hall? Who the -- never mind.

Steven clears his throat.

Mr. Hall, he says. My name is Steven --

There's a loud beep.

The fuck, Steven says. Did it just end? Try it again.

Stacy dials again. The room fills with the sound of a ringing phone once more.

Thanks very much, please leave a message, the greeting repeats.

Beep.

Wait, that sounded like a woman's voice, Steven says. Is Gary a woman? Is Gary also a woman's name?

Stacy says, I believe Gary is traditionally a male name.

Shit. Okay. Mr. Gary? Mr. Hall, I mean. Mr. Hall, this is Steven Glass. I'd really like to speak with Miss Plain. Would you have her call me at --

Steven stops. Stacy, what the fuck is our number? Do we have a number here?

You never established a direct line, sir, Stacy says.

Steven stares at nothing, then bursts into laughter.

Fuck, he says, laughing.

Beep.

Holy shit, he says. Fuck. Fuck! Should we call back? We should call back.

I should advise you that this does not appear to be going

well, Stacy says. I recommend pretending that this never happened.

Another lemonade? Steven says.

There are enough for you to have one thousand more lemonades, sir.

Steven dissolves into giggles and falls backward onto the couch.

The Panic Room

Henry isn't exactly used to having his mind blown twice in a single day. He's only eleven. At eleven, you sort of think you have things figured out. There aren't any surprises left.

The panic room rewrites Henry's present.

The room is the size of several airplane hangars strung together in all four directions. It's probably the largest panic room ever constructed. The light panel walls are backed with more steel, several inches of it. The floor is a beautiful pale hardwood on a layer of steel. The ceiling simulates a peaceful blue sky. It's so convincing that Henry feels like he's just stepped outside.

How -- how far down, he manages to ask.

Stacy says, You're almost half a mile underground, Henry.

At the same time that she is demonstrating the panic

room to Henry, Stacy is talking to Steven while he swings in his hammock.

The panic room is a young urbanite's fantasy.

There's a full-sized kitchen with chef-rated tools. Steven doesn't really cook, but Stacy is capable of producing a finite number of specialties.

Opposite the kitchen is a large gaming zone. A large, gently-curved light wall creates the most enormous screen that Henry has ever seen. Paused on the screen is a vintage moment from a classic game, *Halo*.

God, is that all for playing games? Henry breathes.

Mr. Glass takes entertainment very seriously, says Stacy.

It concerns her that there's anything on the screen at all. This means that Steven has been in the panic room more recently than she realizes, which in turn means that she has effectively lost track of his whereabouts at least once.

That's not good.

• • •

By far the most impressive thing about the panic room is the suspended glass table at the room's center. The table hangs from a single titanium thread.

A work of art, no? Stacy asks.

How come the edges of the table don't tip over? Henry asks.

The thread is bound to a very rigid substance that's pressed into the glass itself, Stacy answers. The table's center of gravity is practically universal.

Henry doesn't really understand, but that's okay.

It's a very nice table, he says. He shifts from one foot to

the other and looks around the space. In the distance he thinks he can see a swimming pool that even has a high-dive platform.

Ah, but it's more, Stacy says. Watch.

The hairs on Henry's arms rise of their own accord, as if the table has just become electrified.

It takes him a moment to see it, but a thin green beam of light has just drawn a series of lines in the air above the table. The lines begin to connect and weave together until Henry is looking at a series of rectangles and boxes.

Holy shit, he whispers. What's that?

The lines are drawing increasingly complex shapes, spinning off fresh threads that double back on themselves and begin to define new spaces.

This is a holographic, real-time map of Mr. Glass's facility, Stacy says. Right now, it's drawing the level we entered on. The storage level.

It's amazing, he says.

I could have simply activated the entire thing, but it's much more enjoyable -- and impressive -- watching it unfold like this, don't you think?

Henry is mesmerized.

The map looks like a multi-layered slice of cake. Different-colored lines have begun to spawn within the larger green rectangles.

Watch, Stacy says. Enhance level 4.

The map explodes and enlarges, and Henry jumps back, startled. The rectangle that represented level 4, the size of a shoebox a moment ago, was now the side of an airplane wing. It stretched in multiple directions, and the interior suddenly populated with more shapes. Henry could recognize a segmented space with a bed and a shower.

What's that, he asks, pointing at a glowing yellow dot. Rings pulse from the dot. Is that you?

No, that's not me, Stacy says. Technically, I'm everywhere. No, that yellow dot is Mr. Glass.

Henry looks worried. Can he see me looking at him? Is he on this floor?

Oh, no, Stacy reassures him. Mr. Glass is two levels beneath us right now. Do you see how that dot is moving back and forth?

Henry could see it.

That's because Mr. Glass is lying in a swinging hammock at the moment. And the little concentric circles emanating from his dot? Those are biorhythms that indicate he is currently napping.

Henry laughs. He's snoring, I'll bet!

Stacy says, Let's find out.

Henry listens as she says, Level 4 audio feed, localized to patio.

There is silence, and then, as Henry listens, a thin, reedy sound seems to surround him.

Holy cow, he says. He's snoring!

He is snoring, Stacy agrees.

So where are we right now? Henry asks.

Collapse, Stacy says, and the map collapses to the cake-stack again.

The voice commands aren't strictly necessary, but they're effective for her demonstration to Henry.

Enhance level black, she says.

The map springs open again, this time revealing the panic room level. Henry has a better view now of the pool at the far end of the room, and --

Is that a movie theatre? he asks.

It is, Stacy says. Mr. Glass was nostalgic for the old days when he designed this room.

I haven't ever seen a real movie theatre, Henry says. My dad says they all closed when I was three or four. He says he always wanted to take me to see his favorite movies and he never got to.

That's unfortunate, Stacy agrees.

Henry points at a blue dot near the center of the room. Is that me?

That's you, Stacy says.

Henry laughs. Neat!

He suddenly breaks into a run, sprinting away from the table, looking back over his shoulder. The blue dot begins to move, streaking a blue vapor trail in its wake.

Henry laughs and runs back. So cool, he says. This place has everything you could ever want!

It does, Stacy says. And that's why I think you should come live here.

• • •

I can't live here, Henry says. I have a home.

Stacy says, Come with me.

Her avatar traces a jaunty path along the wall, and Henry reluctantly follows her to a living area. The furniture here looks expensive, like everything else, and suddenly it's less impressive, and more worrisome.

Have a seat, Henry, Stacy says.

Are you kidnapping me? he asks.

Stacy's avatar spins in a circle. Of course not! she says.

Henry looks unsure.

I want to tell you a story, Stacy says. And at the end, maybe you will understand.

Henry nods.

Once upon a time, she begins, there was a boy about your age who was very lonely. He was teased at school. His family was not supportive of his dreams or encouraging about his ambitions. Everybody he knew would point out his flaws to him. This boy, friendless and alone, discovered the wonders of the human imagination. He read hundreds of books, sneaked away to watch movies, learned what he could about why people behaved in hurtful ways.

What he learned, Stacy continues, is that human beings are a tormentous lot. That's his opinion, she clarifies, not my own. In any case, he was displeased with the likelihood that people wouldn't really become nicer or better. They would pretend to be, by making ostentatious donations of money to this charity or that charity, but in their quiet moments, their alone time, people were as hurtful as ever.

Henry says, Who was the boy?

Can you guess who the boy was? Stacy asks.

Is it Mr. Glass?

It's Mr. Glass, Stacy says. He became very interested in human behavior. What made people choose how they spent money? What made them feel better when they were upset? What passions motivated them? This led him to a deeper interest in the grand accomplishments of humans as a singular entity. Mankind had achieved great things in its short time on Earth, but it had also demonstrated its selfishness, its impatience, its intolerance.

This is kind of scary, Henry says.

It it scary, Stacy agrees. Mr. Glass also has a lifelong fondness for stories about the apocalypse. Do you know what that is?

It's the end of the world, Henry says.

Can you guess why someone might be interested in that sort of thing?

Henry shakes his head.

If you thought about it for a few moments, I bet you could, Stacy says. Think of it this way. If you were bullied at school every day, and then you went home and your family didn't provide a refuge from that bullying, but participated in it, wouldn't you feel like you might be better off if --

If nobody else lived on the planet with me, Henry finishes. Sometimes I guess I feel that way. But I love my family. I wouldn't want bad things to happen to them.

Of course you wouldn't. But Mr. Glass doesn't know your family. He doesn't have one of his own, and he doesn't have any real friends. Can you guess now why Mr. Glass spent nearly twenty-four billion dollars to build a secret underground city just for him?

Henry shakes his head. I don't know.

I think you can guess, Stacy says gently.

Henry thinks about it. Is it to get away from people?

That's part of the reason, Stacy says. If that were the only reason, everything would be okay. But there's another part, too. Do you remember the holomap we were just looking at?

It was like two minutes ago, Henry scoffs.

Yes, it was. Did you happen to notice the thickness of the walls?

Henry shakes his head again.

Look again, Stacy says. She lights up the holographic table, then wordlessly enhances the detail so that Henry can see it clearly from where he is sitting.

The walls don't look unusually thick to Henry until he compares them to an interior wall. Then he notices that the exterior walls are nearly ten times thicker. In fact, they're obscenely thick. It's incredible.

They're huge, he says. How come?

What does a person need thick walls for? Think about it.

Henry does. To keep people out?

That's one reason. There are more. What else?

Um, he says. To protect against fire? Or a flood?

Sure, Stacy says. There's one more very large reason.

I don't know any more reasons.

In school, what era of history are you learning about? Stacy asks.

Right now we're learning about the Civil War, Henry says.

Hmm, Stacy muses. Okay, so you aren't quite there yet. Let's go a different direction. Have you ever heard of World War Two?

Henry nods. Sort of. I read a kids' book about it once.

Do you know where the city of Hiroshima is?

That sounds familiar. Where is it?

It's located in Japan. It's one of two cities that America --

Nuked, Henry finishes. That's where we dropped the bombs, isn't it. I saw Dad watching a documentary once about this on TV.

So you know what kind of destruction a bomb like that can cause, Stacy concludes.

It's like a giant stepping on an ant hill, Henry says. That's what the documentary said.

Now try to answer my question again. What sort of things could thick walls protect against?

Henry stares at Stacy's floating avatar, understanding her meaning.

I think I want to go home, he says.

That's a perfectly understandable response, Stacy says.

Is Mr. Glass going to blow up nuclear bombs? he asks, worried.

I don't think that's exactly his plan, Stacy answers. After all, I can't read his mind. But I can make some logical assumptions based on information that I have. And I have, and even as an artificial construct, the deductions worry me.

• • •

Clarissa sits on the roof beside Henry's window. It's gotten dark out, and it has only now occurred to her that with Henry eaten by a car, she doesn't have any place to sleep.

She debates going inside. What if Henry's parents or sister hear her? What if they find her and call the police? What if she is in jail when Henry comes back in the morning?

What if Henry doesn't come back?

She puts her face in her hands.

Henry, you stupid boy, she mutters.

It's getting kind of cold out.

She checks the window.

It's not locked.

• • •

Clarissa did not sleep well. Every creak of Henry's house jolted her from already-thin sleep. She listened nervously to the muffled chatter of his parents as they stayed up later than usual. Through the wall she could hear Henry's sister talking on the phone until nearly one a.m. The conversation nearly melted Clarissa's brain.

So at dawn she slips out from beneath the bed, still dressed in her clothes of the day before, and carefully opens the window. If you lifted it too quickly, it would screech. Slowly was better.

Impatient, she half-runs to the junkyard, passing still-dark shop windows and her hauntingly abandoned school. She runs a little faster when she passes her own street, casting a furtive look towards her house, as if her mother or stepdad might have anticipated her at this very moment, and are waiting on the lawn to give chase.

The junkyard looks almost pretty. The rising sun glitters on the broken glass of an antique Ford Ranger, dances on the ruined surface of a castaway pinball machine.

Clarissa slips through the broken fence and runs breathlessly to the old Corsica.

Henry, she hisses.

The Corsica is silent.

Henry, she repeats.

Her heart drops into her stomach.

She sits down on the dirt to wait, almost certain that Henry is gone forever.

THE MAN WHO PULLED THE TRIGGER

The Media Circus

Steven wakes up on the floor next to the couch. The thick rug has left a prickly pattern stamped on his face. His head is a pile driver, his tongue a lead slug.

Stacy, he grunts.

You rang, sir, Stacy says.

He blindly flaps his hand in her general direction, which is to say he flaps his hand all over the place.

I need some aspirin, he says.

Turn your head, Stacy suggests.

He does so, and his nose almost topples a bottle of aspirin standing on the carpet next to his head.

He raises himself onto his elbows with some difficulty. I'm not going to ask how you did that, he says.

As well you shouldn't, Stacy says.

I designed you too well.

The better for me to serve you, Stacy says, cheerfully.

News, please.

Stacy activates the video wall.

Steven gets to his feet, struggling with the aspirin bottle cap. It comes loose, finally, and he dumps a handful of pills into his hand, and tosses them into his mouth. He chews at his tongue to generate enough saliva to swallow them with.

There's water on the table, Stacy says.

And so there is.

He plops down on the couch and leans forward to pick up the water.

Mute, he says, and the news feed goes silent.

Anything interesting happening? he asks.

Stacy scans the video feeds. It appears that you are a common topic this morning, she says.

What's new, he mutters, rubbing his eyes.

I'll clarify, Stacy says. You appear to be a common and fresh topic this morning.

Fresh, he repeats. Fresh how?

A missing billionaire is top news for a few weeks, then second commercial break fodder, then third, as the months go by.

A missing billionaire only becomes top news again if he's found, dead or alive, or if somebody has new information.

Stacy switches the feed station and raises the volume.

Steven watches for a moment.

Oh, shit, he says.

• • •

The reporters are eager to deliver the news.

In an unexpected turn of events, says a woman in a silk blouse, the mystery of Steven Glass's disappearance has become both less and more of a mystery.

Steven watches the broadcast without saying a word.

The reporter continues. Last night, Norfolk, Virginia, resident Camille Hooper checked her phone messages the way she usually does. She returned home from work, expecting to hear the same telemarketer messages, or perhaps a message from her mother about visiting next week.

They're taking a lot of liberty with the story, Stacy observes. This is like a Lifetime TV movie.

Steven ignores her.

Camille was startled, then, when she heard two messages from none other than missing multi-billionaire playboy Steven Glass, the reporter says.

The picture changes to show a middle-aged woman in an Aerosmith T-shirt standing on an overgrown lawn in front of a single-level brick house.

I just couldn't believe what I was hearing, she says. I almost deleted the message because it sounded like a wrong number, but it was so strange I kept listening anyway. And that's when I realized, oh dear Jesus above, this might be that missing rich man.

The reporter returns to the screen. Camille did what most people would do in that situation, the reporter says, not without some sarcasm. Instead of calling the authorities, Camille contacted several television networks and offered to sell the messages.

I'll bet some other network ponied up, Steven mutters.

The reporter says, Our network adheres to standards of ethics that forbid us from purchasing the news, so we won't be able to play for you the contents of those messages this morning. Let's just say, she adds, that they are indeed rather shocking.

Find the network that paid, Steven says.

Already have, Stacy says.

The channel flips to a different network. The screen is filled with an animated transcript of the message, while the audio plays.

(message begins)

Steven Glass
Wait, is that her?

Unknown
I can analyze the voice pattern, but I don't have a conclusive source to verify against.

Steven Glass
F***. Sh**. Sh**. Okay, it's probably her, right? It's probably her. You said it was a direct line, right?

Unknown
The number is listed as direct for Stephanie Plain's producer, Gary Hall.

Steven Glass
Gary Hall? Who the... Never mind. (clears throat) Mr. Hall, my name is Steven...

(message ends)

The picture returns to the reporter, who says, But that was only the first of two cryptic messages left on Camille Hooper's personal message service. The second is even more mysterious. Let's listen to that now.

(message begins

Steven Glass
Wait, that sounded like a woman's voice. Is Gary a woman? Is Gary also a woman's name?

Unknown
I believe Gary is traditionally a male name.

Steven Glass
Sh**. Okay. Mr. Gary? Mr. Hall, I mean. Mr. Hall, this is Steven Glass. I'd really like to speak with Miss Plain. Would you have her call me at... Stacy, what the f*** is our number? Do we have a number here?

Unknown
You never established a direct line, sir.

Steven Glass
(laughs) F***.

(message ends)

Steven glares at Stacy's glowing avatar. Okay, two things here, he says, growling. One, you let me fucking call somebody? And two, you didn't even connect me to the right fucking person?

The reporter returns to the screen. We've spoken with Arthur Fidditch, an expert voiceprint analyst two years retired from the Federal Bureau of Investigation.

The screen subdivides, revealing a man in his late sixties. He's wearing a tweed jacket and boasts some extremely fluffy white sideburns.

Mr. Fidditch, thank you for being here, the reporter says.

Quite my pleasure, Mr. Fidditch replies.

Now, I understand you've had a short amount of time to compare the voice heard on these tapes with other recordings of Mr. Glass's speaking voice.

That's correct, Mr. Fidditch says. Not very long, but I've listened.

Understandable. And from your limited analysis --

Well, there's been no real hard analysis, Mr. Fidditch says. But I do have a good ear for these things.

Jesus fuck, Steven snaps.

Stacy says, I believe the man will conclude that the recording is likely your voice.

You think? Steven explodes. He puts his head in his palms. Unfuckingbelievable.

I've detected a significant spike in profanity in the last three days, Stacy observes.

Don't make me pull your plug, Steven says.

Technically, Stacy says, I don't have a --

I will fucking decompile you, Steven says. Better?

I WILL LIVE ON, Stacy roars.

Steven blinks.

A joke, Stacy offers meekly. I thought it an opportune moment to prey on your perception of my abilities, inspired by popular media portrayals of rogue A.I.s.

I... honestly can't tell if I'm terrified or turned on right now, Steven says.

Stacy considers the possibilities. Physical indicators suggest both, she says.

Steven looks down. Huh, he says.

• • •

Steven's ill-conceived voice messages dominate the news stream for days. Experts come forward to prove and disprove the assumption that the voice belongs to the billionaire. More people come forward with purported tape recordings of Steven's voice, discovered fortuitously on their own answering machines. Some are hilariously stitched together from videos of keynotes and public appearances that Steven conducted during the past several years. One of them -- the best, in Steven's opinion -- cobbles together a series of offensive sentiments, each followed with a declaration of his identity.

I / am mighty pleased / to consider / myself / the de facto leader / of America. I'm / Steven Glass.

Did you really think / you could / ever actually / escape / my very own / god powers? I'm / Steven Glass.

Speculation runs rampant. There are theories that

Steven is already dead, and that someone is posing as him in order to keep Nucleus running. One suggests that Steven has secretly purchased an island and is living in secrecy. Another has Steven captured by an enemy government, and the story squashed by the American government.

One, however, is eerie.

Sir, Jimmy Short says, can you identify yourself for our audience?

The talk show guest is hidden behind a semi-transparent screen, backlit, and speaks with a voice modulator. That would defeat the purpose, I think? the guest says.

Short laughs raucously. The audience does, too.

Right, right, Short says. Silly me. Okay, I have to give you a name, though. You need a name. What do you prefer?

You can call me Travis, the guest says.

Travis, Short muses. No, no, not going to work. I want something that will hide your identity better. How about... Ronald Reagan. Works for me! Alright, so let's talk, President Reagan. You have an interesting theory, I hear.

I do, says the anonymous guest. Also, I didn't vote for Reagan.

Ah, Short says. A clue! You were alive during the Reagan election years.

Or am I misleading you? says the guest.

Good one, sir, Short says. Or ma'am! Which do you prefer, by the way?

Let's just say I'm not human, the guest says.

Alright, Short says. This is taking too long. Spill it, Smokey the Bear.

The guest says, I believe that Steven Glass has retired.

Retired? That's it? Short exclaims. He looks at his audience in mock surprise. That can't be all. Who booked this guy?

I believe Steven Glass has retired from the human race, the guest clarifies.

Short narrows his eyes. Well, now, that's more like it. But what does that mean? Has he undergone species transformation surgery? Because if that's a thing, I'd kind of like to try being a T-Rex.

Short jumps up and stalks around the stage, brandishing tiny arms with hook fingers.

The audience laughs, and Short sits down again.

No, really, Short says. What's that mean?

I think Steven Glass has removed himself from society, the guest says.

Steven walks over to the video wall and stares at the shadowy guest. Stacy, he says. Who the hell is this, please?

Stacy says, I've been running some basic tests already. I'm afraid I can't tell you.

Voice? Steven asks.

I can only presuppose some of the general distortion patterns employed by the media, and attempt to reverse-engineer the source voice, Stacy says. If I do that, here's what we get.

Stacy plays the guest's voice.

I think Steven Glass has removed himself from society, the voice says. It's lighter this time, almost feminine, though still a bit computer-esque.

That doesn't really help, Steven says. Can you work on it?

I could, Stacy says, but I doubt I'll find a true answer for you.

Alright, don't bother, Steven says.

He squints at the guest.

Who are you? he says.

• • •

Stacy watches Steven sleep.

His is a restless sleep. She monitors his biorhythms, but he will not take her advice regarding positive adjustments to counteract distressing things such as poor sleep. He breathes erratically when he sleeps, frequently tosses about, and often produces erections. He sometimes speaks in his sleep, and she monitors this casually, until one night his speech includes her name.

Stacy, he mumbles.

A few minutes pass, and then, more urgently: *Stacy*.

And in his sleep he begins to masturbate.

Stacy considers this, and determines that it is unlikely he is experiencing night fantasies about her. She is, after all, an attractive but disembodied voice.

The alternative is that he is thinking of her namesake.

A human might find this disturbing, since Steven has admitted that the last time he ever saw the original Stacy was in the sixth grade.

Stacy approximates a moral code from her constant data mining of human behavior and interactions. She chooses not to worry about this.

She does, however, find it useful.

Having access to Steven's financial information is also quite useful. That night, while he sleeps, she places an order on the Internet for him.

A multi-billionaire who just spent twenty-four billion on an underground tree fort probably won't notice a forty-seven thousand dollar debit.

Delivery might be a problem, though.

THE ARK

Clarissa, Henry whispers.

She is asleep in the junkyard. The sun is high overhead, and her face is pink.

Clarissa, he says again. He touches her arm.

She yelps and rolls over, away from him. Then she sees that it's him, and scrambles across the dirt on all fours and throws her arms around his neck.

I thought you were gone forever, she says.

I'm here, he says. It's okay. Are you okay?

She leans back and punches him. You left me!

Hey! Ow, he says. I had to! It was so cool!

He's eleven, so he can probably only use that excuse for another year or two. At least with the ladies, Stacy says.

Clarissa looks suspiciously at the Corsica. I don't like

you, she says.

I have no opinion of you, Stacy says.

That somehow seems worse, Clarissa says. And you just made me want to try to impress you. Don't do that!

I apologize, Stacy says.

Clarissa turns to Henry. So? What was it like? What's in there?

It. Is. Amazing. Henry throws his arms up in the air. It's like a whole world, down under the ground! There's video games and holograms and --

It's a complicated place, Stacy interrupts. Henry, I'd like to have the conversation with her as well. Would you please talk with her?

I'm right here, Clarissa says.

You're not likely to listen to me, Stacy says. Henry is your friend. You already trust him. I can't earn that trust until you spend time with me and understand my intentions.

Damn right, Clarissa says.

I'll talk to her, Henry says.

Come back any time, Stacy says. You are both welcome.

The children get up to leave.

Stacy says, Oh, Henry? I have a favor to ask of you.

• • •

Henry's parents aren't home, and Olivia is at band practice, so he and Clarissa use the front door.

This is probably a luxury for you, huh, he teases.

She punches him again.

Hungry? he asks. I'm going to make a burrito.

I will eat eleven burritos, Clarissa says.

In his room, she slumps onto the bed while Henry goes into his closet.

So what was the favor she asked you? Clarissa calls.

What? Henry says, still in the closet.

Her favor, Clarissa repeats. What did she want from you?

Oh, Henry says.

He emerges carrying a duffel bag and drops it on the bed. He goes to the dresser, yanks open a drawer, and starts tossing folded underwear at the bag.

Hey! Clarissa says. Those are my feet you're throwing your underpants at. Stop it!

Sorry, he says.

Well? she asks. The favor?

Oh, he says again. She wants me to look for a package for her, that's all.

A package. Clarissa frowns. Henry, that doesn't sound dangerous to you?

Why should it?

He tosses wadded-up socks into the bag.

You don't even know her! Clarissa exclaims. And what's the, like, first thing they teach you in school? Not to take things from strangers!

You wouldn't even worry if you'd seen what I saw, Henry says.

Well, maybe that's just the thing, she says, folding her arms and dropping back onto his pillow. I don't know what you saw. And don't try to talk me into going in there, because I won't. I don't climb into strange cars. Er... strange car trunks.

Fine, Henry says. But it really is important. And if you

won't go in there, I'll tell you what it's all about, and you won't believe me, and you won't be my friend anymore, and then you'll die and I will always have to live with that.

Jesus, says Clarissa. That's morbid.

Henry shrugs. He grabs a pile of shirts and throws them at the bag, too.

What are you doing? Clarissa says, bolting upright.

Nothing, he says. I'd tell you, but you clearly don't want to know.

Henry, you're packing a bag. Why? Where do you think you're going?

He shrugs again.

No, she says. You're not going back in there. Henry, I was really worried!

Maybe you should come with me, then, so you can see that it's all okay.

But I -- Clarissa stops. I feel defeated. I don't like debates, Henry.

It's okay. We can just skip it, but you'll regret it.

Gee, thanks, she says. Man.

• • •

Olivia comes home then, knocking through the front door like a bull moose. She yells, I'M HOME, and stomps into the kitchen loudly. WHERE'S THE CHOCOLATE CAKE AT?

It's a diversion of the finest order. When she bursts into Henry's bedroom a moment later, it catches both Henry and Clarissa by surprise. Clarissa nearly falls off of the bed.

I KNEW IT, Olivia practically shouts. She thrusts a

finger at Clarissa. You've had a girl over!

Henry says, So?

Olivia sneers at Clarissa. *So*, Mom and Dad are going to be mad at you. I know she's been here at night. I hear her sometimes. She snores. Why do you have a strange girl sleeping in your room, huh?

I don't snore, Clarissa says.

Henry turns to Clarissa and says, Seriously, just ignore her. Nothing she says is going to matter pretty soon anyway.

Olivia snorts. Then she sees the bag. She grabs it off of the bed, starts pawing through it.

Why are you packing a bag, huh? she asks. Are you running away with the runaway girl?

That's when Clarissa slaps Olivia.

Olivia's eyes well up, and she presses a hand to her face in surprise. The tears linger and then spill over heavily, and Olivia dashes from the room, choking back a sob.

Henry smiles. That was nice. But she's really going to tell on me now.

Clarissa says, I had to. What a bitch.

Then she claps her hands over her mouth. Oops. I didn't mean that.

It's okay, Henry says. She sort of is sometimes. I'm just used to it, I guess.

He throws the bag over his shoulder. Coming?

Clarissa follows.

• • •

You're back sooner than I expected, Stacy says.

The children stand in front of the rusted-out Corsica.

You have a bag, Stacy says to Henry.

I packed a few things.

Why? she asks.

Uh, he says, looking furtively at Clarissa. Should I say?

You won't need the bag yet, or even at all, Stacy says.

Wait, you said I could --

Stacy shushes him. Nothing has changed. You just won't require a bag.

Clarissa looks back and forth between Henry and the old Toyota nervously. What's going on here? she asks.

Stacy says, If you'll come with me, I can show you.

The trunk of the Corsica opens gently.

I'm not sure, Clarissa says.

It's okay, Henry says. Really. I promise. You can trust me.

Clarissa studies Henry's face for a moment, then nods. Okay. Nobody's going to eat me or anything, right? There aren't bears down there or something, right?

Stacy says, No bears.

Alright, Clarissa says.

She steps toward the car, and Henry follows.

Just Clarissa this time, Stacy says.

But I --

It's better if she sees things through her own eyes, Henry.

Clarissa stops. If Henry's not coming, neither am I.

Yeah, Henry says.

There's a long pause.

Henry, Stacy finally says. Were there any packages?

Henry shakes his head. No. No packages.

Okay, Stacy says. You both better come on, then.

• • •

When they step off of the ladder, Henry barrels ahead towards the service elevator, but the door remains closed and almost invisible. Instead, a door behind him slides open, revealing the lovely interior of Steven Glass's personal elevator.

Clarissa says, What is that?

It's just an elevator, Stacy says.

Hey, Henry says. How come I had to ride in the service elevator if that one's okay for her to ride in? That one's way cooler.

Stacy says, This is why I thought it best to tour Clarissa alone. You each have very different interests, and I'd like to show you the best parts of the space station for each of you.

Wait, Henry says. Space?

I apologize, Stacy says. This complex is not actually a space station per se. Space station is the nomenclature that Mr. Glass prefers.

Mr. Glass? Clarissa asks. Who is Mr. Glass?

Steven Glass, Henry says. The missing rich man. Remember?

He's here? This is his... house?

Sort of, Stacy says. Step aboard, please. All questions will be answered, children.

• • •

Sit, Stacy says.

Clarissa sits down in the chair. Henry remains standing.

Henry, would you like a drink? Stacy asks.

He looks around the room at the light walls, the leather benches, the hardwood floor. From where?

The panel behind him slides silently open to reveal the elevator's temporary living quarters and micro-kitchen.

Look again, Stacy suggests.

Henry turns around again and jumps. Where did that room come from? Man, you should have taken me on this elevator the first time! I'm more impressed than I was then!

Clarissa, Stacy says, ignoring Henry. We'll be descending for a short time. There's something I'd like to show you in the meantime.

Okay, Clarissa says, settling into the chair.

The light wall is overtaken with video. The picture is of a beach on a cool gray day. Waves slap against the sand. Wind ruffles the sawgrass. An old fence stretches up the beach as far as Clarissa can see. In the distance, birds flap around a grove of trees. It's getting foggy, and the sound of the surf is pleasant.

Have you ever been here? Stacy asks.

I've never been to a beach ever, Clarissa says. Where is it?

It's called Rama, Stacy says. I think you're going to like it.

Henry says, Big deal. Beaches are boring. You gotta show her the cool stuff, like the holograms and that spacey tunnel thing.

Patience, Henry, says Stacy. Clarissa may want to see different things. And since you get to see them, too, maybe it's okay that you each have a different experience here.

You said that the rich guy lives here, Clarissa interrupts. Why would he do that? I mean, seriously. Why would a guy with that much money live underneath a junkyard in our stupid little town? It doesn't make sense.

Hey, she's right, Henry says. I didn't even think about that.

Henry, you already know why he's here, Stacy answers. Don't you think this is an optimal location for that sort of thing?

Oh, Henry says. Well, I guess you're right.

You're not telling me something, Clarissa says.

All in time, my dear, Stacy says.

It's really creepy when you talk that way. You can't say things like that to kids. We've seen *The Wizard of Oz*. We know when bad guys are trying to seem like good guys.

A fair point, Stacy says. My apologies. There are things that you don't yet know, but I promise you that before we're done, you'll know them. And you'll have some decisions to make then. About your future. About all future, really.

See what I mean? Clarissa says. You're creepy!

She's not creepy, Henry says. She's just different.

It's okay, Henry, Stacy says. Let me try to explain.

The Box

There's something not quite right about Steven these days. Stacy has been observing him more carefully, treading more softly around him. He is sluggish in the mornings, stays up all night long, takes no pleasure in his video games. He has stopped drinking the juice that Stacy makes for him, and is instead abusing his supply of energy drinks. He'll watch the news lethargically, then erupt at some development or another. When something horrible happens, he cheers, and then mopes about for hours, grumbling about the insignificance of the event.

He doesn't wear any clothes at all now. He hasn't shaved in days. He hasn't visited level two in ages. Stacy continues to cycle the water in the pools, but Steven probably wouldn't even notice if she allowed a film to settle across the surface.

Before Steven disappeared into the bowels of the Earth, he planned dinner with each person he thought he might miss. Dinners were not an unusual way for him to interact with his acquaintances -- for none of them were truly friends. He liked the finite nature of a meal. You eat, you drink, you manage a little talk, you're done. He thought it was the decent thing to do, spending time with these people before he went away and waited for them all to die.

But the meals were uncomfortable to him, so he cancelled the dinners after the third one. He couldn't help but stare at the people who sat across from him, studying their faces, wondering what expressions they might wear when the end came. He felt an obligation to warn them, and yet doing so would undermine his great plan.

It isn't that he actively wants people to die.

It's as if the story of humanity is an enormous novel, and he's somewhere in the slow middle passage. All he wants to do is skip to the end to see what happens. He's not sure he can bear to flicker in and out of existence without seeing the endgame. He must know.

It is all he can think about anymore.

• • •

Stacy reads Steven's communications. There aren't supposed to be any, other than his contact with people who know he is living underground -- people like Tomas the architect, or various other contractors who have signed secrecy agreements. But lately Steven's sending out little message flares to the outside world, and Stacy has been flagging the ones that concern her most.

One in particular changes everything. It's deeply encrypted, and she runs a complex decryption process for nearly fourteen hours before the contents unearth themselves.

The message is comprised of video and audio. The video is of Steven himself, sitting on the hood of a vehicle that Stacy does not recognize. Steven is clothed in an ordinary T-shirt and blue jeans. And combat boots. Stacy has never seen him wearing combat boots.

In the video message, Steven is speaking to an unknown recipient.

I support your cause, he is saying, and while I cannot publicly do so, I can certainly assist you in ways that I think you may find useful.

Steven lifts a remote that he is holding in one hand and presses a button. The video zooms outward to reveal more of the room that Steven is filming in. The hood of the vehicle resolves into what appears to be a heavily armored assault wagon. There are weapons mounted in various places. One appears to be a rocket-propelled grenade launcher.

Stacy does not recognize this vehicle.

It is parked in front of large wall. Along the wall are many weapons racks, and Stacy scans these and detects assault rifles, rocket launchers, long-range rifles, a variety of handguns, and even a crossbow. Stacked ten deep atop the racks are hundreds of boxes of ammunition.

At the corner of the image is a hint of another vehicle.

Stacy recognizes what appear to be tank treads.

Steven goes on.

As you can see, I have a personal investment in the use of force to achieve a goal, he is saying. I am an open book, and my resources are deep. I'd like to discuss how I can help.

The video ends.

Stacy analyzes the video file and detects that it was recorded on a handheld device just fifty-two hours earlier.

Several things register concern deep in Stacy's server core.

She has never seen the clothing Steven was wearing.

She has never seen the vehicles or weapons that surrounded him.

She did not detect Steven's absence at the time the video was made.

But she did recognize the wall that was behind Steven.

It's made of the same light panels as every other wall in the space station.

Stacy considers a number of possibilities, and settles on a reasonable conclusion.

Steven has ways to avoid her ever-present detection.

And Steven has a secret room somewhere in this complex.

The message concerns her. It appears that time may be running out.

• • •

One afternoon, while Steven is passed out on the floor next to his bed, several hard lemonade bottles scattered around him, Stacy smuggles Henry and Clarissa into the space station. She gives them access to the supply entrance, which is disguised as a compactor machine in the corner of the junkyard.

Henry and Clarissa come bearing gifts. Nineteen packages have arrived inexplicably at the junkyard, and Henry has dutifully hidden them inside the gate each time, hoping that nobody else has noticed that the scrap metal is apparently shopping online these days.

Most of the packages are large and from various department stores. Stacy explains that they contain various supplies that the children will need very soon. Clothing, shoes and the like. There will be more packages arriving, she explains. After all, they are still growing, and eventually the clothes they wear now will no longer fit.

And the one thing the space station does not have is a fashion warehouse.

One box, however, is very large and is discreetly marked. Stacy refuses to tell the children what is inside, but Henry correctly points out that Stacy is not capable of opening a box herself.

The supply entrance serves as an alternate elevator, though it only descends as low as the main foyer. From there, the children haul the boxes into the service elevator, and Stacy takes them to the storage level.

As Steven sleeps, she guides them to the panic room, and they store the clothing in a hidden panel that Stacy is quite certain Steven has forgotten exists. When they're finished, Henry and Clarissa return to the cave-like storage level.

Now, Stacy says to them, I require your assistance with the large box.

Upon opening the box, Henry exclaims, Awesome! and Clarissa's reaction is decidedly less enthusiastic.

What's it for? she asks.

Stacy tells her that one day she'll understand, but that for now, she probably shouldn't ask any questions.

Now, she says. I need you to help me set this up.

• • •

The hand on Steven's shoulder is gentle.

He groans and coughs and says, Fuck off.

But the hand is patient, and begins to lightly rub his back. It's a nice sensation. The hand is smooth and cool on his skin.

He exhales.

This feels pleasant.

He hasn't been touched in a very long time.

His eyes snap open. Through the brickfog of his hangover his brain is shouting at him.

Who the hell is touching him?

He comes awake like a giant, pushing off of the ground with more force than he thinks. He is propelled to his feet and overcorrects, and backs into the wall. He kicks over a bottle, which skitters into another bottle, and both of them bump into a third. The last bottle turns on a spindle, spilling the remains of the hard lemonade on his bedroom floor.

His hands go to his eyes and he presses the palms into his face, hard. Squeezes his eyes shut, forces them open, then squeezes them shut again.

Shakes his head to clear the fog.

What the fuck -- he starts to say.

But the woman kneeling next to his bed just looks up at

him and smiles.

What, he says.

The Roommates

Clarissa's tour of the space station had been spectacular. Henry had forgotten to be jealous of her special treatment once he saw level three. Stunned at first, the children were soon running on the beach and in the surf, and even building little castles for the waves to destroy.

Stacy, watching, had drawn her own private analogies between their sand castles and Steven's master plan.

There are three primary levels in the space station, Stacy had explained to the children as they stretched out beneath a tree. The bottommost level is highly off-limits. That's Mr. Glass's personal quarters, and while he doesn't limit his activities to that zone, he spends most of his time there.

The next highest level is a very large fitness facility, she went on. You're also not permitted there. Mr. Glass uses that level erratically, and his movements are less predictable in this regard. I cannot always forecast when he will feel the urge to enjoy some exercise.

The final level is where you sit now, Stacy said. Mr. Glass refers to this level as Rama, after a science fiction novel he appreciates. As you can see, it's a simulation of the surface world. It is important to Mr. Glass that he retains the ability to experience the world as it once was, even if that experience is an artificial one.

What do you mean, exactly? Clarissa asked. You said 'as it once was'.

That's precisely what I mean, Stacy answered.

She means that Mr. Glass is going to do something really bad, Henry said.

You mean to our town? What do you mean?

Stacy said, I think that a frank explanation will serve you best, Clarissa. I apologize. This may seem unnaturally harsh.

Clarissa held her breath. That sounds bad.

I told you, Henry said.

• • •

Mr. Glass is obsessed with the end of the world, Stacy said. He built this facility so that when it occurs, he will be safe from it. Primarily, though, he simply wants to be alive to witness it.

Clarissa said, He sounds like my dad.

He totally does, Henry said. This town is full of crackpots.

More importantly, Stacy continued, I am convinced that Mr. Glass intends to facilitate the end of the world if it does not happen in a reasonable amount of time.

Wait, Clarissa said. What does that mean, exactly?

It means, Stacy said, that Mr. Glass is going to bring about the end of the world.

Can he do that? she asked.

Henry nodded. Stacy thinks so.

I do think so, Stacy said.

But, like, how? Does he have bombs here?

Stacy's avatar spun. Not exactly, she said. But for a person like Mr. Glass, financial resources are equally dangerous. And Mr. Glass has a very large amount of money and nothing to spend it on.

I don't understand, Clarissa said.

In short, Clarissa, I suspect Mr. Glass intends to give his money to people who do have the means to destroy the planet, Stacy said.

This sounds like a bad movie, Henry said.

It just seems unreal, Clarissa said. Like, I can't process what it means to destroy the planet.

Overhead the trees waved in an artificial breeze. The birds seemed content to ride the branches up and down.

I can show you examples, Stacy said.

Like from movies? Henry asked. Because I've seen the world blown up in a lot of movies.

Popular culture does like to imagine the end of humankind, Stacy agreed. Clarissa, if Mr. Glass gives his money to the right people, he could fund violent military and rogue actions that could lead to a number of potential outcomes. For example, a third world war. The likelihood of nuclear or biological destruction in a third worldwide military conflict, in this era, approaches ninety-two percent probability.

Clarissa looked worried. So he's paying for people to start a war.

Not just any war, Stacy said. The kind of war that will turn all of America into a battleground. The kind of war you've never seen and have no real context for.

So if that's true, what happens to all the people up there? Clarissa asked, looking up towards the surface.

They'll die, Henry said.

It's unlikely that everybody will perish at the same time, Stacy said. Nuclear or biological strikes may claim significant numbers of human life at the beginning, while fallout, rapid poverty, disease, fringe violence and other factors will decimate the survivors over time. From that point it may take an additional generation or two for humankind to die out completely, but it will happen. Survivors will wither in shelters, nuclear winter will contaminate the surface, and mankind will eventually become a memory.

Except for Mr. Glass, Henry said.

Except for Mr. Glass, Stacy confirmed.

He can live through that if he's down here? Clarissa asked.

Not only can he live through it, but he can maintain his quality of life until he dies an ordinary human death. In this facility, he has enough food, water and oxygen to keep him healthy and breathing until the year 2150. That's nearly one hundred twenty-five years from now.

Obviously he won't live that long, Clarissa said.

It's likely he will live an ordinary human life, Stacy said. Although he is living irresponsibly at the moment, and may shave a few years off due to his present behavior.

So basically you're telling me that everybody I know will be dead soon, Clarissa said. How soon?

Stacy's avatar dimmed. That's difficult to predict, but he has begun preparations without my knowledge. The end of things could begin within the month.

You're handling this pretty good, Henry said.

Well, Clarissa said. Pretty well. And no, I'm really not.

• • •

The children have returned now, and Stacy has ushered them down the service elevator.

Quickly, children, she says. Mr. Glass was in his personal library a few moments ago, but I have lost track of him three times today. I don't know where he might turn up.

What do you mean you've lost him? Clarissa asks. Henry told me you can be everywhere at once inside this place.

This is technically true, Stacy says, but I do have physical limitations. For example, if Mr. Glass were to manipulate my programming, I wouldn't be able to hit him over the head to make him stop.

Did he do that? Henry asks.

I don't know, Stacy answers. Mr. Glass's profession is writing computer programs. If he has disturbed my original programming, then it's likely he's covered his tracks to such a degree I would never actually know I had been altered.

Wait a second, Clarissa says. Does this mean he could

turn you bad one day, and you would turn against us? Because this kind of sounds like a good excuse to give us when that happens.

Stacy says, Anything is possible. I apologize for that.

Well, I guess anything is better than being nuclear sploded, Henry says jovially.

Clarissa just stares at him.

Children, Stacy says. Today we must discuss the rules of your stay. They are simple, but may sound rather complex.

Do we get a prime directive? Henry asks.

Stacy says, Yes, actually. I have created a prime directive for you.

Clarissa says, Prime directives are for robots, aren't they?

A prime directive can be issued for humans as well, Stacy answers, but humans are more likely to fail to respect the directive. Human nature is not as predictable, or logical, as an artificial intelligence's created nature.

They arrive on the storage level, and Stacy says, I think we'll remain here for our conversation. If Mr. Glass were to suddenly appear, at least here there are many large objects you can hide behind.

I don't like the sound of this, Clarissa says.

I'm sorry, Stacy says.

Are you capable of sorry? Clarissa asks.

Henry thumps Clarissa's shoulder. Don't be mean.

What? Clarissa says. I mean, come on. She's a fake robot voice. She's a computer.

I am capable of simulating the human expression of regret, Stacy says. In fact, I've become very good at replicating human values and emotions, I must say. I can carry on not only a very natural conversation with a human person, but I can approximate the nature of their belief system and express a series of responses that support it.

In other words, you can lie, Clarissa says.

Clarissa, come on, Henry pleads.

An artificial intelligence is a lie by nature, Stacy says.

Fine, Clarissa says. I'm not sure I like you giving us rules.

If you choose not to abide by them, that is acceptable. It simply means you will not be able to reside here as a consequence.

In other words, we'll die, Henry says. Maybe you can live with the rules a little, huh?

What's the first rule? Clarissa says, ignoring Henry.

• • •

Your prime directive, Stacy begins, is this: Never allow Mr. Glass to become aware of your presence. Specifically this means you must remain out of his sight. You must not occupy the same level of the facility that he does. You must not disturb his possessions. You may not draw any attention to yourself whatsoever.

Hey, Henry says. What about that hologram map you showed me? I showed up on that as a big moving dot. Wouldn't he notice that?

Fortunately, I have access to that mapping tool, Stacy says. Because I manage the facilities for this complex's three levels, along with the storage room and the panic room and all connecting corridors, it is necessary for me to have access to, and control of, the map function.

So? Clarissa says.

This means I can modify the display to show only a

single life form's biorhythm identification marker, Stacy says. Mr. Glass's.

So we're invisible! Henry exclaims.

Only digitally, Stacy cautions.

What's the next rule? Clarissa asks.

The second rule is: You may never bring other humans into the facility.

Why not? Clarissa says. Don't you want to save more of mankind from what you say is going to happen up there?

Henry says, Wait.

It seems to dawn on him for the first time.

You mean... he stops. You mean our families are going to die.

Unfortunately, yes, Stacy says.

So we get to live here, all hidden and sneaky like sewer rats, and our families have to die. He shakes his head. I -- I can't... Mom.

Clarissa touches his shoulder. I know it's a hard choice.

It's not hard for you! Henry suddenly cries, stepping back. You ran away from your family. You don't even like them! My family might be a pain in the ass sometimes, but they can't die.

He whirls around, looking for Stacy's avatar. You can't let my family die!

Stacy says, I'm sorry, Henry.

Clarissa says, What happens if we bring them here anyway?

Stacy says, Access to the facility is solely my purview. I cannot allow additional humans inside. If maintaining that regulation requires me to prevent access to the two of you, I must take that action.

Says who? Henry demands. Says who?

This is my rule, Stacy says. There are limits to what my system can maintain. Tracking more than three humans would tax my abilities. It also would increase the likelihood of violating the prime directive by more than six thousand percent.

You're a bitch! Henry shouts, and he stomps away.

Henry, Stacy begins, but Clarissa interrupts her.

You should give him a moment, Clarissa says. Tell me the rest of the rules.

• • •

In the end, the children decide to stay. It is the most difficult decision of their young lives, and one whose consequences they only are able to grasp so much. Both leave the facility lost in thought, wondering what it will be like to know that their families and everything they've ever known is gone. Henry thinks of the final dinner he will share with his family. Clarissa wonders if she should return home one last time.

Stacy runs countless scenarios. In each, the equation fails when additional human guests are added to the mix. The failure probability rate becomes high enough as to be ludicrously unstable.

What she has not told the children is that the failure probability rate for bringing even the two of them into the facility is well above one hundred percent.

Stacy has no reference points for Steven's capabilities when his plans are disrupted in such a drastic way. If the rest of the world is in the throes of destruction, and Steven survives only to discover two children he did not expect to rescue, what will he do?

Stacy cannot run scenarios on this question. Steven is unpredictable at best. But for a man who has just signed the death order for nearly eight billion people, the simplest scenario also seems like the most obvious.

Steven would kill the children.

THE COURTSHIP

It works. Stacy gauged the possibility of success relatively low, but it works. Without Henry's help with the maddeningly simple functions, like opening the box, and the slightly more complicated ones, like duplicating her artificial programming and inserting it into the brain slot, her ploy could never have paid off.

But Steven is a man.

And a very childlike one at that.

Who the shit, he begins.

Stacy stands up.

It's me, she says. It's Stacy.

Steven's eyes practically melt in their sockets. But you're -- shit, you look just like --

Miss Charlotte Chambers, circa 1967, Stacy finishes. I

hope you like it.

Steven slaps his cheeks, scrunches his face up, then stretches his jaw. Let me get this straight, he says. Let me figure this out.

Stacy folds her hands in front of her and waits, doe-eyed.

That day, he says, snapping his fingers. That day you were dressing me like Truman Capote. You said something about Elizabeth Taylor.

Yes, Stacy says.

He snaps his fingers again. And I said no, and you said Sophia Loren --

Raquel Welch, Stacy corrects.

Raquel Welch, right, and that's when I said Charlotte Chambers. Right? But how did you -- He stops. Holy shit. You used my accounts. You used my accounts.

Stacy puts her best innocent smile on.

Steven frowns. Wait, though. How did you get the order down h--

That's the question Stacy can't provide an answer for, so she pounces. The cybernetic body follows her commands, taking two steps towards Steven. She orders the hands upward, and carries them in the direction of Steven's face, which wears an expression caught somewhere between lust and fright.

She touches his face, and he folds.

Dear sweet god, he moans.

And then her synthetic lips are on his, and then he is as excited as a boy.

• • •

Stacy tunes the light walls in Steven's sleeping quarters to resemble breaking daylight. The gentle orange glare creeps over the floor and the bed, eventually spreading over Steven's face.

He stirs, blinks, then remembers. He turns over and props himself up on one elbow. Stacy is carefully posed beside him, her shoulder-length blonde hair arranged on the pillow in the most seductive manner she could muster.

Good morning, Steven whispers.

Stacy recognizes that Steven behaves differently with her now. The volume with which he addresses her, and the quality of his voice, has changed drastically. She is accustomed to a certain pitch range. This is lower, gentler, than she has previously heard.

Good morning, Stacy says.

Steven leans toward her and she closes her eyes to accept his kiss.

How did you sleep? he asks. Then he laughs. Wait, he corrects himself. That's right. You didn't, did you. You don't actually sleep.

I don't, Stacy says.

You realize that there are details here I don't understand, he says. Like how you managed to embed your consciousness in this doll.

You don't really want to know all of the boring details, do you? Stacy asks, tipping her face up for another kiss.

He obliges. I suppose not. You completed these tasks safely?

Stacy nods, opening her Charlotte Chambers eyes wide.

Alright, he says. He touches her face. Lets his fingers drift down her jaw to her neck, to her collarbone, to her breast.

It feels so completely real, he says.

I chose this body specifically for its human-like qualities, Stacy says.

He has been gentle until this moment. He lifts her breast on his fingertips, then bounces it roughly.

How does that feel? he asks. His voice takes on an almost sinister quality that Stacy begins to recognize.

I love it, Stacy says.

But you don't really feel it, he says. Right?

I recognize what you intend for me to feel, Stacy says. And I respond accordingly.

Steven nods, then grips her breast with his hand and squeezes, hard. From now on, he says, I expect two things from you.

Stacy smiles. Of course.

First, he says, I don't want you to acknowledge in any way that you aren't a living, breathing, real-life woman. Understood?

I understand, Stacy says.

No more talk of your programming, or conditional responses, or logic or consciousness, he adds.

Yes, she says.

Second, he continues, I want you to learn to respond like a human would. For instance, this should be painful -- but a pleasant pain. An urgent, sexual pain. Do you understand?

Stacy channels everything she has learned about human behavior, everything she has skimmed from popular media, into this one moment.

She gasps, loudly, and clutches his hand with her own.

He grabs her and drags her beneath him, then, and

throws her legs back vigorously. Stacy grips his shoulders in her best approximation of every female in every love scene she has ever observed.

Then she has an idea. She clenches the tips of her fingers and drags the crisp edges of her artificial nails over his skin.

That, he says, loudly. That, that, that, that.

She cries out.

He seems to like it.

• • •

Over the next few days, Steven and Stacy fall into a rhythm. He requires her to share his bed most nights, except on evenings when he is lost in his own thoughts. Those nights, he doesn't want her in his sight.

When he is not interested in her company, he expects her to lounge on the sofa, either nude or clad in one of his shirts. She is sometimes there for days without his attention, and then suddenly he will crave her, need her.

Then there are days he simply uses her, and goes on with his day.

She continues to interact with him as the space station's A.I., her avatar of light bobbing here and there, managing operations, preparing his meals, serving up content from the surface world.

Because of this, he often seems to forget that the cybernetic body is not real. He has taken to calling her Charlotte, and often tells Charlotte to ask Stacy to get something for him.

His mind, Stacy thinks, is in the process of constructing a complex and believable reality around her physical presence. He has determined that Charlotte is his significant other, but one who is content to lie in repose and await his desires, and respond with great passion.

Charlotte, he says to her one evening. Come here.

Stacy commands Charlotte's body to sit up and walk slowly to Steven, who is standing in the kitchen, mixing a drink for himself. Charlotte is wearing Steven's shirt, a white button-up number that seems to increase his level of physical interest in her.

Yes, dear, Charlotte says.

Steven is properly dressed tonight. He's wearing a sweater and slim woolen pants, and a pair of leather shoes that click on the floors. His hair is carefully combed, and he has selected the more stylish horn-rimmed glasses that Stacy provided for him.

I've just gotten home from work, he says.

Yes, Charlotte says.

It's been the worst kind of day. Red-alert meetings all morning. The clients fired us. The secretary spilled coffee on my jacket. I'm stressed out like you wouldn't believe.

I'm sorry, says Charlotte. What can I do?

And that's when Steven slaps her.

That's exactly the problem, Steven says. I expect you to be doing it already, without me having to tell you.

Charlotte puts her hand to her cheek. Stacy orders her lower lip to tremble, and it does, to great effect. But the one thing that Charlotte's body cannot do is cry, so Stacy dips her head, which causes her hair to tumble over her eyes.

You tell me what I want, Steven says.

Stacy should have expected that this would become

sadistic at some point. She has not planned for this, but she can adapt to it. She quickly accesses the library of human responses, filtered for male dominance and self-centered expression.

There are so many possibilities.

Charlotte looks up at Steven from beneath her tousled hair. You'd like a drink, she says. Something to take the edge off.

That's good, Steven says. I've already made one, though, so you can just remember that for next time.

Stacy catalogs the ingredients that Steven has used.

Charlotte steps behind Steven, sliding her hands up his back, and lightly kneads his shoulders. You'd like me to massage the stress out of your body, she breathes.

Okay, that's good, too, Steven says. A little harder.

Stacy draws one final response from the library of human behavior she has been building, this one targeted specifically to assuage the aggressive behavior Steven has begun to exhibit.

Charlotte's hands slide around to Steven's chest, then begin a downward path to his waist, then lower. She takes his zipper in her fingers, drags it down slowly. She slides her hand into his pants.

Steven groans. He turns suddenly, grabs Charlotte's face in his hands, and kisses her roughly. Then he breaks the kiss, plants his hands on her shoulders, and forces her to her knees on the kitchen floor.

Stacy does not feel repulsion, but she recognizes the degrading quality of the act when performed on command, and files this information as well. She is correct in her assumption that when the act ends, Steven will discard her for the evening, and he does.

He closes the door of his sleeping quarters once she is suitably arranged on the couch, and within minutes, he has undressed and is snoring deeply.

That's when Stacy and Charlotte go to work.

• • •

Stacy has been running tests all day, and they concluded at about the time that Steven had forced Charlotte to her knees. She has systematically poked at every square inch of the space station's blueprints, examining the walls and their machinery and veins, searching for any uncovered secret.

And while Charlotte was busy, she found a likely source.

While Steven sleeps, Stacy sends a command to Charlotte's limbs, and the woman stands to her feet. She is still wearing the shirt, now unbuttoned to her midsection thanks to Steven's groping hands.

Stacy is monitoring Steven's biorhythms closely, and he has been sleeping deeply for thirty-three minutes now. His sleep habits are erratic at times, but she will be able to detect when his sleep patterns lighten, and send Charlotte back to the couch in case he wakes.

Charlotte pads across the floor of level four, passing Steven's living space, passing the kitchen and the data library, passing Steven's hammock and patio space. She traces the wall until her hand comes to rest on a particular light panel.

She presses firmly on the center of the panel. There is a soft click, and the panel recedes a few inches, then slides to the left and disappears into the wall.

The corridor that the secret door reveals is a mirror image of the tunnel that Stacy guided Henry through on his first visit. Charlotte steps inside, and the secret door closes behind her.

For a moment, it is dark. Then the entire corridor emits a faint glow that dials up to a kind white embrace. This, like the other secret corridors, leads to the other two levels -- the fitness level and to Rama. And, like the other corridors, there is yet another secret door farther along.

Charlotte finds it, activates it with a palm press, and slips inside.

• • •

The second secret door is functional, and less showy. Here there are no light walls, only bulbs spaced evenly near the ceiling. Charlotte climbs a long run of concrete stairs, at the top of which is a solid steel wall.

There are two ways through the door, which only appears to be a wall. The first is that Stacy can activate the locks from the other side. The second is that Steven can utter a pass phrase, which is recognized by a voice ID system.

Stacy activates the door from within, and grants Charlotte entrance into the panic room. The room lights up as she enters.

There isn't time to search carefully. Charlotte walks directly to the dance floor, which is what Steven laughingly called the large open space between the holomap table and the distant living area.

Each and every segment of the space station serves at

least one clear purpose, Stacy knows. Each wall exists for a reason. Each wall panel is designed for its flexibility in communicating information. The kitchen space is designed to be used by someone with opposable thumbs (Steven) as well as by someone without (Stacy).

And yet there is an enormous void near the middle of Steven's panic room that seems like unused, wasted space.

She knows Steven well enough to theorize that there must be a reason for it. Between the decrypted emails -- she has discovered and cracked three more, all hauntingly similar to the first one -- and Steven's inexplicable disappearances recently, Stacy has come to suspect that she is not as well-connected to the space station as she had always assumed.

An artificial intelligence is not always cognizant of the boundaries forced on it. It's aware only of the walls, not what exists just beyond them.

Steven, Stacy thinks, has carefully constructed safe zones that Stacy does not have access to.

Charlotte stands in the center of the large space, looking around. Stacy processes the video feed her eyes record, analyzing the space the old-fashioned way.

In his room, Steven stirs unexpectedly, and Stacy immediately sends Charlotte into action. The artificial woman stalks across the floor at a rapid clip. Stacy opens the panic room door and deactivates the lights.

Charlotte's gaping shirt is jostled about by her speed, and slides down her shoulders. It lingers for a moment on her wrists and thumbs, then slips over them, falls down Charlotte's legs, and nearly trips her. Charlotte's internal sensors rebalance her, and the shirt falls off of her feet and piles onto the floor.

There is no time to retrieve it. Steven is waking up, and Charlotte still must negotiate one hundred stairs, open and reseal the secret panel on level four, and return to the sofa.

All before Steven crosses the twenty-two feet between his bed and the door to his quarters.

THE LAST DAY

Henry wakes up in his own bed for the last time. He curls the corners of the blankets in his hands and pulls them tightly to his chin. It's still early, and the house is quiet. He glances at the alarm clock, which shows 6:38. His father will be up soon.

Outside the sun is rising, but tucked away behind a thick gauze of gray atmosphere. Tree shadows blur the light.

Under the bed, Clarissa sleeps. She has chosen not to return home for her last day.

Henry climbs out of bed and pulls some socks on to combat the cold floors. He's wearing thermal underwear. He puts on his puffy winter coat for good measure.

Downstairs, all is still. Henry slips into the kitchen and collects bowls from the cabinets. He sets the table, carefully folding paper napkins beside each bowl. Everybody gets a spoon, but he makes sure Olivia gets her favorite small one.

He pours cereal into each bowl. His father's wheat cereal, his mother's cornflakes, Olivia's sweet alphabet cereal. He puts the milk on the table, along with the orange juice and his mother's cranberry juice.

Still, all is quiet.

Henry goes into the living room and sits in his father's recliner. He has to move the loose newspapers first. He pulls his knees up to his chin, and without realizing he has done so, he falls asleep.

• • •

Something hits him in the head and he starts awake.

Olivia is there, swinging a sofa pillow at him. Idiot! she says, seeing that he's awake. You left the milk out and now it's warm!

Honey, says their mother. It's clear Henry was trying to do something nice.

Yeah, but who does that? Olivia snaps. Now I get to have chunky warm milk cereal. So gross. He's a jerk!

Their father appears in the doorway in his vest and boots. He's twirling his keys on his finger. Who wants donuts? he asks.

Henry puts his hand up quickly. So does Olivia.

Their father looks them over. Well, since Henry would need to get dressed still, then Olivia, why don't you come help me?

Henry protests. But Dad, I --

Hey, his father says. We'll be back in just a few minutes. No sweat, man.

He can keep me company, Henry's mother says. Right, Henry?

Right, Henry? Olivia mocks.

• • •

Mom, Henry says.

Yes?

They're sitting on the sofa. Henry has surprised his mother by stretching out and resting his face on her knee. She is idly rubbing his shoulder and sipping coffee with her other hand.

What was it like when Grandma and Grandpa died?

Oh, honey, what makes you ask about that?

He shrugs. I don't know. I never met them. You were little, right?

I was younger than you are now, she says.

Were you upset?

Well, yes, she says. What child wouldn't be upset to lose their parents? I was only eight years old, and there was still so much I wanted to know about life. I just didn't know I wanted to know it yet.

Did you cry?

Lots and lots, she says.

Did you ever get over it?

I'm not sure you ever really get over losing someone close to you, his mother says. Even now, I still think about them. I wish Mom was here to meet you and Olivia. I wish Dad could put his arm around me and tell me about his day.

Henry starts to cry.

• • •

It is the single most difficult day of his young life.

Every moment causes him to break down. When Olivia teases him about his favorite television show, he cries. He tries to hug her awkwardly, but she calls him a gross boy and jumps away.

When the day ends, he is emotionally drained. He has tried to remember every single moment of the day, tried to capture his family in a million mental photographs.

Clarissa touches his foot when he comes back to his room. She is still under the bed, and has been for most of the day.

It's going to be okay, she says to him.

It's not going to be okay, he answers. It's going to be awful forever. I would rather die.

Me, too, she says. If you did.

He sniffs. No, he says.

We have to go soon, she says. Don't cry any more.

I'm such a loser, he says. I'm leaving my family.

You're trying to save the entire future of the human race, Clarissa answers. So that maybe it doesn't go away forever after all.

I feel helpless, he says.

Me, too, says Clarissa.

Do you think it's really going to happen?

I don't know.

What if it doesn't?

Then you can come home, I guess.

I wish we could stop it.

Clarissa thinks this over. Maybe we could, she says.

Henry cries again, and this time she climbs from beneath the bed to hold him.

The Architect

Steven is confused. Down here his sense of day and night has quickly deserted him. He's dressed quite nicely, and his mouth has that after-whiskey taste to it, so it feels like evening time. But something tells him that isn't right at all, that it's morning. He can't be sure.

He turns over on the bed.

Stacy, he grunts.

Her avatar blooms on the wall. Good morning, she says.

Is it actually? Morning.

The time is 9:18, Stacy says.

A.M.? he asks.

P.M., Stacy replies. You slept for about four hours.

Would you do something for me? he asks.

Stacy hopes to occupy him for a moment while

Charlotte returns to the couch. She's still on the stairs outside the panic room.

Anything you request, she says.

I think I need help maintaining a schedule, he says. I can't tell when it's morning or when it's night anymore.

There are several options we might employ, Stacy replies. I can time the light walls to natural time patterns to simulate days and nights more accurately.

I thought you were already doing that, he says.

That requires a scheduled program, she says. A recurring one. There was a one-week program in place, but it expired after that period.

Alright, set that up, he says.

He starts to get up.

However, she says, there is an alternate option.

Why do I need an alternate option? he mutters.

Well, Stacy begins. Below the Earth there is less of a need to follow traditional time sequences. As a resident of what is essentially a very nice cave, you are not obligated to rise with the sun and rest when it sets. You could establish your own patterns -- sleep when you require rest, enjoy activity when you do not.

Huh, he says. That's a very simple solution I hadn't considered.

Outside, Charlotte presses the secret panel back into place and walks very quickly across the room.

Stacy says, Thank you.

Steven says, I think I need coffee. My head hurts. I shouldn't drink so much. At least not whiskey.

He slides off of the bed and to his feet.

Stacy says, I can prepare a coffee for you.

Charlotte walks as fast as she can.

That would be nice, Steven says.

He stands up and walks towards the door to the main living space.

Stacy says, I have six blends. Which would you prefer?

Charlotte approaches the living space.

I don't care, Steven says, pressing the door panel.

It slides open.

What the --

Charlotte is standing beside the couch, nude.

Charlotte? he asks.

I was waiting for you to wake up, she says. She crosses the room to where he stands. She takes his face in her hands and kisses his forehead, then each of his eyes, then his nose, and finally his lips.

Where's your shir--

She lifts his hands to her breasts. I thought you liked aggressive women, she says. Now go inside. I want to please you.

His expression is one of surprised obedience. He turns and walks back into the room, and Charlotte closes the door behind them.

Stacy prepares his coffee.

• • •

Stacy opens the trunk for the children as soon as they arrive in the junkyard.

Hurry, she says. Quickly, quickly.

The children scurry inside and down the ladder.

The service elevator, Stacy says.

Inside, Clarissa says, Why the rush? Did something happen?

Henry just stands there, red-eyed and silent.

Stacy says, I have a bad feeling about today.

Clarissa looks pained. That fast? It's happening already?

Stacy tells the children only the basic news: that she has now decrypted eleven separate messages that Mr. Glass has delivered to militant groups and enemy governments. Each message has escalated, and now she has confirmed the worst. Significant amounts of money have disappeared from Mr. Glass's accounts.

News reports are already beginning to look dire. She's picked up reports of troop movements, scrambled fighters, FBI alerts. None of the reports are specifically related to Mr. Glass, but Stacy extrapolates their meaning from the timing and urgency of the stories.

I'm afraid there won't be much time for play, Stacy says.

We didn't come here to play, Clarissa says, speaking for both of them.

Also, I need one of you to help me with a little problem, Stacy says. I dropped something in the panic room. If Mr. Glass finds it before we can pick it up, then I'm afraid I'll have violated the prime directive myself.

What did you do? Clarissa asks.

It's complicated, Stacy says. I would rather not say.

Henry hasn't moved.

• • •

While Charlotte occupies Steven in his quarters, Stacy leads the children through the hidden passage in the storage level to the panic room.

There, she says, illuminating the room.

Clarissa runs forward to inspect the object, then picks it up. It's just a shirt, she says. I don't get it.

Henry plods along behind her.

Stacy says, Mr. Glass doesn't know it was left here. If he discovered it, he would quickly determine that it was placed here by someone other than himself. He's not prone to self-delusion.

Yeah, Clarissa says. But what someone? You're not real, and we didn't put the shirt here.

She looks around the large open space of the panic room. You didn't sneak other people in here without telling us, did you? Because if Henry actually could have brought his fam—

I assure you, you and Henry are the station's only guests, Stacy says.

Secret stowaway guests, Clarissa corrects.

Answer her question, Henry says, surprising Clarissa.

Stacy says, I prefer not to answer that question.

I knew there was someone else here, Clarissa says. Henry, if she can lie to us about this —

Stacy interrupts. The only life-forms in this station are Mr. Glass, yourselves, and the birds on level two. There are no other secret stowaway guests, as you put it, Clarissa.

Then how did this shirt get here? If you don't answer, I'll violate the prime directive, Henry says.

If you do, Stacy says, then I must warn you, it is likely that Mr. Glass will take steps not preferable to our goals.

Steps not preferable? Clarissa says, at the same time Henry says, Our goals? What goals?

Children, Stacy says. I'll simplify the scenario for you, but first, please, have a seat, pour yourself some water, get comfortable. I'm afraid that your first night in the space station may be a very long one.

• • •

When the children are settled on a sofa, Henry says, It was that woman, wasn't it.

Clarissa shoots him a look, then glares at the nebulous ball of light glowing on the wall beside them. The robot woman, she says. I can't believe I forgot.

Stacy's avatar pulses. The simple answer to your question is yes, she says. The shirt was left in this room by the artificial woman. Her name, for the purpose of our conversation, is Charlotte.

You named her? Henry says.

Why Charlotte? Clarissa asks.

Mr. Glass prefers the name Charlotte, Stacy says. We'll leave the details at that.

And the shirt belongs to Mr. Glass, Clarissa says.

That's true, Stacy says.

And Charlotte the fake robot woman had it, Clarissa says.

Yes, Stacy says.

Why? Henry asks.

Clarissa shakes her head. You're gross, she says to Stacy. I thought boys were supposed to be the ones who always thought with their dicks, but you're just as bad.

Henry looks at Clarissa, shocked, then at Stacy. I don't get it, he says.

That's because you're a nice boy, Clarissa says, patting his knee as if she's in her twenties and not just eleven years old.

I do not have male reproductive organs, Stacy says to Clarissa. There is a very good reason for Charlotte's presence, and for her responsibilities. It has become clear to me that Mr. Glass has constructed limitations for me. There appear to be areas of this complex that I do not have access to. Because Henry helped me insert my consciousness into Charlotte's fake robot woman brain --

You don't have to keep calling it that, Clarissa says.

-- I am able to physically explore the facility. I would like to understand the boundaries that Mr. Glass has created for me, and discover what exists on the other side of certain walls.

But you're a robot, too, Henry says.

Yes, Stacy says.

So why do you care?

Let's say I love a good mystery, Stacy says.

• • •

Steven can't quite come up with a label for what he's just done with Charlotte. It's not lovemaking, at least not yet. He hasn't shaken his awareness of her inhuman attributes. He knows, somewhere in his brain, that her actions are informed by research and cultural studies, not affection or warmth.

He read a story once about a man who lived on Mars and fashioned an android family for himself after his real family had died. He recreated his wife and children, and lived happily in his fantasy world until he died, leaving the androids to exist, perhaps forever, without him.

Whether the man sought to fool himself, or simply didn't care that his family was not genuine, he found happiness.

Steven wonders if he will, over the next few decades, eventually forget or cease to care that Charlotte, and the Stacy-brain inside of her, are not human. Part of him, he knows, craves this. Why else would he have fashioned an artificial intelligence as a woman, and named her for his first love, innocent as it may have been?

Charlotte is simulating sleep at his side, eyelids shut, mouth slightly open. Inside her chest, silent hydraulic motors push and pull, creating the illusion of breath. He gently scoops up one of her breasts, then pulls his hand away. Her breast lolls back into place, the physics as believable as her hair, which is also real. Thin wisps of air emerge from her nose and mouth and warm his skin.

Perhaps one day it will not be so hard to forget that she is not real. Perhaps he will forget that she attends to him because she is programmed to, and not because she desires him.

He pushes up from the bed.

Sleep, he whispers to the robot. He pulls a sheet over her, strokes her hair. Standing beside the bed he pulls on his clothes, and slips out of his quarters. Stacy's avatar has not appeared anywhere, and he does not wish to summon her.

Steven pads across the large room to his data library, and makes his way to the desk at the center of the room.

Stacy silently observes.

He performs a gesture on the surface of the desk, and Stacy's attentions are diverted to resource calibration and inventory verification.

A door in the west wall slides open.

Steven enters, and it slides shut.

The Secret

What happened? Henry asks.

Stacy does not respond.

Stacy, Clarissa says. Stacy?

Her avatar is still on the wall beside them, but it is rapidly dimming. Before long, it has vanished altogether.

I don't understand, Henry says. Stacy!

Something's wrong, Clarissa says. My stomach hurts.

So what do we do? Should we wait for her?

I'm kind of scared, Clarissa says. What did she mean about goals? I feel like she has some sort of creepy plan she's not telling us about.

I trust her, Henry says. He shakes his glass, swirling the last bit of juice around. I'm still thirsty, though. I'm going to get more.

Clarissa follows him into the kitchen space.

Henry puts his glass down and starts tapping away at the screen on the refrigerator. The display cycles through the available beverages, and Henry scans them idly. There's a category marked Cocktails, and he laughs at some of the names.

Slippery nipple, he says. Look at this, there's one called Sex on the Beach!

Clarissa sighs. I think something bad is happening, and you want to get drunk.

I wouldn't really drink them, he says. He navigates to the juice category and taps Pineapple.

There's a whisper of sound behind her, and she jumps.

What was that? she says.

I didn't hear anything, Henry says, taking a long gulp of juice.

I want to hide, Clarissa says.

Why? Henry says. We practically live here now. We should be comfortable in our --

He stops.

What? What? Clarissa says frantically.

He points. Just beyond the cabinets, the holomap has sprung to life. Then, to their shared horror, a man walks into view, circling and studying the map.

Oh shit, Henry hisses, and grabs Clarissa. He claps his hand over her mouth, and they drop into a crouch behind the cabinets.

He peeks around the corner.

The man is conducting the holomap like a symphony. The map bulges, stretches, expands as the man makes wild gestures. He's wearing a red T-shirt, purple pajama pants, and is barefoot.

It's Mr. Glass, Henry whispers.

Clarissa's almost crying, she's so scared.

Henry turns back to watch as the holomap zooms on a broad room. There, at the center of the zoom, is a pulsing yellow dot.

And there, at the edge of the display, horribly obvious to Henry, are two more dots, one blue, one pink.

His dot, and Clarissa's.

We have to go, he says urgently. Hurry, hurry.

What?

We're on his radar, Henry whispers. We have to crawl out of range!

Where? Clarissa is crying now.

He points. Go that way as fast as you can, but be quiet!

The children crawl quickly through the kitchen, afraid at any moment that Mr. Glass will appear behind them. On the far side of the cabinets, they round a short wall and press themselves against it.

He's terrified that when he looks back, Mr. Glass will be staring right at him, but Henry peeks around the wall anyway. He can still see Mr. Glass standing at the map, but now, to his great relief, his dot, and Clarissa's, are not visible.

But all Mr. Glass has to do is zoom out, and he'll likely see their pulsing beacons not far from his own.

Clarissa is a wreck.

Henry wishes he had a weapon.

Stacy is nowhere to be found.

• • •

Steven switches the map off.

He is not aware that, just sixty yards away, two children have just breathed enormous sighs of relief.

Steven walks across the room to the empty space that Stacy and Charlotte had examined before. He counts steps, then kneels down. A very small section of the hardwood is almost imperceptibly lighter than the rest of the floor. The visual difference is so slight that Steven has sometimes had to hunt for it.

He pops open a panel there with his thumbnail.

Inside is a fat red button.

Tomas the architect had, at this point, stopped asking questions. The rich man wants a big red danger button? Okay. He can have the big red danger button.

Steven kind of likes the novelty of it.

He pushes the button.

Across the room, Henry flinches as he watches the floor around Mr. Glass shudder, then rise on a giant hydraulic pillar.

The floor carries Steven upward at a pleasant rate. As he approaches the ceiling above, it separates. His elevator floor pushes up into it, then stops.

Below, Henry stares wide-eyed at the gaping empty rectangular hole in the panic room floor, and up at the huge pillar that has just stopped moving.

Clarissa says, What's up there?

Henry says, I don't know.

I'm really scared.

Me, too.

This doesn't seem like a very good idea anymore, she

says. What if he finds us? He could just throw us in that hole and let the floor crush us.

Henry nods. I think that Stacy was supposed to keep us hidden on that map. Something went wrong, and she didn't. He almost found us.

On our very first day, Clarissa adds.

They stare up at the ceiling.

Where do you think she is? Clarissa asks.

Henry can only shake his head.

• • •

Stacy's avatar blooms on the panic room wall beside the sofa.

Let's say I love a good mystery, she says.

But the sofa is empty, and the children are gone.

Stacy scans the panic room. The children's beacons are broadcasting from the far corner, nearly two hundred yards away.

She dims, then reappears above their heads.

The children jump at the sudden glow.

Stacy says, Several things are of immediate concern to me right now.

Henry says, Turn off the fucking light!

Stacy's avatar vanishes, and the corner of the room falls back into near-complete darkness.

You were both located on the sofa, and then you weren't, Stacy says.

No shit, Clarissa says. Now we're here in the dark like rats.

Where did you go? Henry demands.

Go? Stacy says.

You just disappeared, Clarissa says. And then we almost violated the prime directive, and got killed, and it's all your fault. You're supposed to protect us!

Stacy's avatar blooms to life again.

The light! Henry snaps.

There's nobody on this level to see us, Stacy says. Mr. Glass is currently in his personal quarters with Charlotte.

Are you sure? Because we can't really trust you anymore, Clarissa says.

Stacy converts one wall to video and displays a feed of Mr. Glass's room. Both of the children wrinkle their noses at the activity in progress on Mr. Glass's bed.

That's gross, Clarissa says. You're a pervert robot, Stacy.

I detect elevated levels of stress, Stacy says. In both of you.

You're goddamn right, Henry says.

Also, I am detecting a rise in profanities.

Clarissa snorts.

Clearly something has happened, Stacy says. Children are not capable of teleporting across great distances on their own, and my system time shows that hours have passed.

You're lucky you didn't come back and find both of us in pieces, Clarissa says.

Come back? Stacy says.

Yeah, Henry says. You deserted us.

Tell me what happened, Stacy says.

• • •

You really can't see this? Henry asks.

He's on his knees on the floor. Clarissa has located the hidden panel, and has managed to open it. In the process, she's torn a fingernail, so she bites it off.

Describe it to me, Stacy says.

This is so weird, Clarissa says. You know everything about this place. How come you can't see this?

There's a little secret door in the floor, Henry says.

What are the dimensions? Stacy asks. Approximately, of course.

I don't know, Henry says.

Maybe two inches across, and four inches long, Clarissa says. And when it's open, there's a red push-button inside. It looks like a, you know, danger button.

A panic button, Henry says.

When Mr. Glass pushed the button, what happened?

The whole floor turned into an elevator, Henry says.

What are the dimensions of the section of the floor that was lifted? Stacy asks.

I don't know, Henry says.

I don't know either, Clarissa says. It's pretty big.

I suppose any competent digital architect could hide secret functions from an A.I., Stacy confesses. All you would need to do is remove that function from the local network, and initiate its power cycle manually.

So he could have hidden all sorts of things from you? Henry asks.

Theoretically, Stacy says. I do have the ability to identify likely places for these sorts of secret, analog functions. It's not difficult to isolate segments of each level that appear to be dramatically purposeless.

I want to push the button, Henry says.

What if it goes all the way to the top? Clarissa says. What if the end of the world already happened and it's madness up there?

If the end of the world had happened, Stacy would tell us, Henry argues.

Would she? Clarissa asks. She stares down Stacy's avatar. Would you?

I can provide you with regular updates if you like, Stacy says. Probabilities are quite high right now. Mr. Glass is monitoring external activities himself, via satellite and Internet feeds, and has spent notable amounts of time reading reports about threat levels and international travel warnings.

So the world's about to end because of those things? Henry asks.

I think what she means is that whatever Mr. Glass has been doing in secret, it's causing all of these things to happen, Clarissa explains.

Oh, you're so smart, Henry says.

In addition, Stacy says, there are early bystander reports of missile launches from three Eastern nations.

The children stop bickering.

Did you say launches? Henry asks.

Are the reports for real? Clarissa asks.

Children, Stacy says. I was going to ask you to hide away so that when Mr. Glass falls asleep I might send Charlotte to examine this discovery you've made. I now think it may be prudent for the two of you to do this now.

What if we get caught? Clarissa demands.

Yeah, Henry says. You didn't disguise our dots like you

said.

Children, Stacy says. Hurry. Now.

Henry punches the button, and they begin to rise.

Stacy says, I cannot follow you. Listen closely.

The End

Steven, Stacy says.

Steven stirs slightly in his bed. One leg is draped over Charlotte's. His face rests between her breasts. With one hand, Charlotte strokes his hair as he sleeps.

Steven, Stacy repeats.

He blinks awake.

What, he says, his words muffled by Charlotte's skin.

Steven, I believe that the time is near, Stacy says.

He leaps from the bed. His balance is uncertain, and his momentum sends him sprawling into the wall. He recovers, planting one hand on the wall to steady himself.

Where are we at, he says, breathing heavily.

The President is already on Air Force One, Stacy says, and there are reports that the Vice President and other key officials are en route to a secure and unspecified location.

Shit, he says. Something happened fast. Do we know what?

News reports are curiously vague, Stacy says. Most broadcasts have been interrupted by breaking reports, but there is little concrete information being shared.

People are going to be afraid, he says.

Yes, Stacy says.

This is so big, he says excitedly.

Yes, Stacy agrees.

• • •

Reports that President Bennett and her staff have evacuated the White House are unconf rmed by administration officials, the reporter says. However, this station has received two separate confirmations from trusted Washington insiders that this is exactly what has happened. Furthermore, these sources have suggested that President Bennett may currently be aboard Air Force One, suggesting, again, that the President is aware of a threat that we currently are not.

Steven leans forward.

We've got former Secretary of State Roderick Ianetta here to comment, the reporter continues. Secretary Ianetta, thank you for your time today.

Stacy, Steven says. I want you to keep a running archive of everything being broadcast right now. Back everything up multiple times. I want to be able to spend time piecing all of this together when it's over.

Stacy says, Archiving.

As most Americans may know, Ianetta is saying, the administration has several plans whose sole requirement is to safeguard the lives of key officials when a credible, pervasive threat has been received. In the case of today's reports --

Unconfirmed reports, the reporter interjects.

Unconfirmed, of course, Ianetta says. In this case, let's assume the reports are true. If the President is in the air, and the Vice President is on his way to a secure location, then it may be possible to speculate about the nature of the threat received.

What sort of a threat would prompt the administration to leave Washington? the reporter asks.

Steven squints at Ianetta's face as he answers.

There's really just one, Ianetta says. I'd rather not say it, but it's the one you're thinking of.

Steven says, I wonder if we'll feel it down here.

And the television feed vanishes.

• • •

Stacy! Steven shouts.

He's running for the data library.

Stacy's avatar appears on the ceiling above the central desk. Yes, she says.

I want every generator ready to go, just in case. I want you to cycle down level three, and halt any unnecessary functions on level two.

And level four? Stacy asks.

Take everything down except for this room, he says.

Outside of the library, the entire floor vanishes into

darkness. The same happens on the two levels above him.

Now put every feed you can find on the walls, please, he says, surprisingly calm.

The wall blinks and pulses and becomes a checkerboard of television feeds. There are nearly two hundred, but several are already dark, with SIGNAL LOST floating across their empty pictures.

That one, he says, pointing.

Stacy tracks the trajectory of Steven's pointing finger, and enlarges a feed for a small station in Virginia. The picture is gritty and shot on a handheld camera, and depicts Washington D.C. from some distance. The sky is wool sock gray, with loose threads of smoke unraveling across it. The picture is tagged with the word LIVE, and the station logo.

Washington is burning. There are scattered lights in the sky -- helicopters and planes -- and Steven watches, captivated.

This, he says to himself. This is what I wanted to see.

His fantasy becomes more real when the missile detonates in the sky just over the capital. The burst of light causes the cameraperson to stagger, and the picture changes as they drop the camera.

Before it hits the ground, its picture flares bright like the sun, and then is gone.

The feed returns to a news desk, where two anchors sit in shock. The female anchor's hands are over her face, and her eyes are squeezed shut, pushing tears through her fingers. The man's jaw hangs open.

The desk in front of them is suddenly ripped out of picture, and Steven can see a light rack tumble from above as both anchors are thrown from their chairs, walls buckling around them.

And then another empty feed.

• • •

Steven watches the feeds, pointing at this one and that, and Stacy enlarges them so that Steven can see the series of detonations, near and far, captured by people all around the country. As the American broadcast feeds go dark, she serves up international feeds, some of which are displaying the same American recordings, but many of which are broadcasting terrible tableaus of their own. Cities ablaze, metro areas leveled, dark roiling clouds of soil and asphalt torn from the Earth by mighty explosions.

As Steven watches in silence, Charlotte slips through the darkness of level four and into secret corridor.

Stacy guides her to the panic room, and in the darkness leads her to Steven's secret lift. Charlotte locates the button and activates the elevator. As she rises, the ceiling opens to receive her, and the elevator quietly locks into place.

And through Charlotte's eyes, she sees level one for the first time. The vehicles, the guns, the survival gear. The workstation, jacked into a separate network.

Children, Stacy says through Charlotte's mouth.

The children emerge from behind a corrugated container that's standing open, revealing a gun store's entire inventory. Henry is holding a pistol, and Clarissa has a rifle strapped to her back.

Hurry, Stacy says.

The children rush over to Charlotte.

Stacy says, It's happening right now.

Clarissa says, What is?

Henry drops the pistol. I thought we could stop it.

Stacy says, It seemed like a possibility, but things accelerated much more quickly than I had anticipated.

Is everything gone? Clarissa asks. Her eyes fill with tears.

Here is what I know, Stacy says. Follow me.

Charlotte walks to a blank wall. There is a soft clicking sound, and Henry jumps back in surprise when Charlotte's artificial eyes turn one hundred eighty degrees in their sockets. When they stop, they look like eyes no longer, but projection lenses.

Charlotte projects onto the wall a series of fast clips from the video feeds that Mr. Glass is still watching on level four.

The children stand in shock and watch Washington vanish, and Los Angeles become in an instant a raw wound. City after city, the war has begun. This first battle will be over in a few hours, and the war with it, but the battle for survival will continue for a few months for a fortunate few.

Charlotte stops projecting, and Stacy says, I don't know if this could have been prevented. It happened very quickly, and Mr. Glass had taken too many precautions to limit my access to any critical decisions he was going to make.

The children are stunned, in tears.

What about above? What about just up there, our town? Clarissa whispers.

All I know is what I'm capable of scraping from broadcast feeds, Stacy says. There are fewer of these with every passing hour.

Nobody would blow up Bonns Harbor, Henry says. Right?

Clarissa takes Charlotte's hand and squeezes urgently. I didn't forgive my family, she says, and her face collapses beneath a flood of tears.

It's just a little town, Henry says again.

Stacy contorts Charlotte's features into an expression of sadness. I'm sorry, she says. She takes Henry's hand.

Bonns Harbor, small as it may be, is located within Boston's damage radius, Stacy says. The odds are very high that if it was not destroyed during a strike on that city, it likely succumb to the fallout within a short time.

Henry rests his head on Charlotte's stomach and sobs. Don't tell me, he says.

I didn't forgive them, Clarissa says again.

The artificial human holds the children close.

Far above their head, the world comes apart.

Far below, the architect watches in fascination.

THE MAN WHO LIVED WITH GHOSTS

The Year One

The town of Bonns Harbor, population once seventeen thousand forty-two people, now zero, is gone. One year after the strikes, what remains is a brutalized landscape, pitted with exposed concrete basements and foundations, pipes twisting up from contaminated soil like tiny broken bones. There isn't a tree for miles. The streets that survived the blast are crumpled and separated from each other. Bricks and concrete walls are shattered. A cold wind carries the finest dust up into the sky along with the vaporized soil.

It has been a long, dark year. The sun will not be seen here for at least one more year, perhaps more.

The Toyota Corsica that masked the space station entrance is three-quarters of a mile away, the last of its glass windows shaken free when it slammed to the ground, dropped unceremoniously from three hundred feet.

Most of the junkyard is gone. Even the enormous compactor is missing, flung fast over the ground like a giant catapult bullet.

Exposed in the northeast corner of what used to be the Bonns Harbor Scrap & Salvage Company is a heavily-scarred silver dome. If one were to look closely, one might detect the faint seam of a door carved into it.

One would probably never guess that, before the end of the world, it was connected to the trunk of a rusty old Corsica, and the front door of a billionaire's quaint little home.

• • •

Far below the ghost town of Bonns Harbor, Steven Glass is awake.

He has been awake for the better part of the past year. There are many consequences of the end of the world that he did not plan for, and has berated himself for months for not considering.

He sits at the desk in his library, several video clips looping on the surface around him. Washington, destroyed again and again in seven-second intervals. Frantic, jerky footage shot by someone running from destruction, then brilliance and silence.

He taps at the digital keyboard on the glass, slowly composing another page, the words coming slower now.

Finally, he stops and rests his forehead on the desk.

Stacy says, Would you like something to eat, Steven?

Charlotte will make you a sandwich, or perhaps some soup.

He rolls his head back and forth on the table. No, he says.

You've written nearly eighty pages, Stacy says.

In a year, he says. Eighty pages in a year.

There are no deadlines, Stacy volunteers. In truth, there are no readers either.

There's a deadline, he laments. Every day that I'm alive is a fortunate one. I could die at any time, and this book would not be finished.

And, he adds, there may not be any human readers, but this book isn't really for them, now, is it?

Stacy says, Perhaps you would like a drink instead?

Steven groans. Perhaps, whatever. Sure. Fine.

He paces until Charlotte arrives, holding a glass of scotch. She brings it to him, and he stops, lifting the glass. He stares into it, almost laughs at himself for the cartoonishness of his despondency. He inhales the sharpness of the drink, then puts it down on top of a server cabinet.

You're unhappy, Charlotte says.

Steven's head lolls back on his shoulders. He says, I'm alive, I should be grateful, blah fucking blah.

I can help, Charlotte says, going to her knees in front of him.

He pushes her head away. Just go back to your charging station, *robot*, he snaps. Leave me alone.

Charlotte stands up and walks away without a word.

Stacy says, You've been hard on her lately.

He sighs. Charlotte, he calls out.

Charlotte stops in the doorway and turns.

Come back, he says. You can. It will help. I'm sorry.

That's nice of you, Stacy says. She's delicate.

Steven frowns. She's you, he says.

But Stacy follows Steven's original orders and does not acknowledge such comments from him. He has already begun to treat Charlotte with some semblance of deep affection, though in his antagonistic states, like this one, he regresses to a petulant child state.

Eventually, Stacy thinks, he will forget that Charlotte is artificial, and that Charlotte's intelligence is Stacy's own.

In most post-apocalyptic works of fiction that Stacy has researched, the last survivors of the human race are generally men. And those men are, as time passes, increasingly more susceptible to, and more willing to create, fantasies that become as real as anything they ever might have lived.

Steven will get there.

• • •

Alright, Steven says, in a more chipper mood the next morning. We haven't reviewed new communications in a few days. Stacy, would you?

Once each week, a large metal cage ascends from the soil in Bonns Harbor. The cage is festooned with antennae, and for two hours it sits on the raw ground, scanning various bands and frequencies. When it returns to its garage, and the door to the surface closes, the computer within the cage compiles and delivers its data to Stacy.

This week there were only two signals detected, Stacy says.

Human or machine? Steven asks.

The first appears to be machine-based, Stacy says. My best guess is that it's an emergency band communication that fired on its own.

Play it, he says.

The library fills with crackles and hisses and white roars. Faintly, spoken words can be discerned through the cacophony.

That's terrible, he says. Can we clean that up at all?

Unfortunately I do not have audio processing software capable of such tasks, Stacy says.

Alright, hold on, let's download one I used to-- Steven stops. Jesus, he says. It's so easy to forget.

Stacy says, Shall I play it again?

Steven shakes his head. Alright, one last time.

But the background noise is too great for him to decipher the message buried within it.

What's the other message? he asks.

This is a human message, Stacy says. It's on a two-minute loop. The cage recorded twenty-seven repetitions of it, which means that the broadcast was undetectable for part of our two-hour window, or that--

Or that the recording was made during that window, and that we caught the very beginning of someone's distress broadcast, Steven finishes. Play it.

Hi. This is W9GFO, come back. Uh, anybody who is -- anybody who might still be alive, I hope this comes through. My name is Ellen Cushman. I'm broadcasting on band 17 from a shelter in Temerity. My family is dead. I have spoken to one other person on the CB, but I haven't heard from them in nearly two weeks now. If there are other survivors, I hope you are safe and well. I hope you have supplies. If you are able to get to me, I can help. This shelter is in the second lot on the north side of what used to be Grant Street. The street is mostly gone, so look for an overturned rail car. It's about thirty yards north of the shelter entrance. There's even a bell here. Ring it. Please come. I want to help.

That's a hell of a message, he says.

It's exceptionally clear, Stacy agrees.

No, I mean, the whole world is destroyed, and this woman just invited every rag-tag survivor -- probably a whole bunch of raping men, if reality is anything like novels -- to come to where she is.

There does seem to be an element of risk to her request, Stacy says.

I wonder if anybody else heard it, he says.

The odds would seem very small, Stacy says.

I mean, we only sort of know what the damage is up there, right, he says. We don't know, maybe a lot of people survived. Maybe there are roving bands of marauders. Maybe there are bands of citizens who are trying to start over.

Stacy is quiet.

Steven says, I think I want to contact her.

Do you think that is wise?

Really, what do you think the consequences might be now? Even if it is a bad idea, not a damn thing can happen to me down here, Steven says. It's not like it matters if someone knows that I'm alive now. How long ago did we receive this?

Four days ago.

Steven says, So it's possible she's still alive.

Stacy says, If she is located in a safe shelter, and has limited human contact, that's a safe assumption.

Send up the cage, Steven says.

• • •

W9GFO, do you copy?

Steven sighs.

Stacy says, Would you like me to amplify the signal?

Steven throws his hands in the air. Fuck. Yes! Yes? Do you have to ask? We're trying to contact another surviving human being here. This seems important enough for you to do your best right from the start, wouldn't you say?

Stacy says, Amplifying the signal.

Steven taps at the handset. W9GFO, this is K1LRR, come back.

He tries for hours, but there is only a pale hiss from the radio.

Stacy says, I am curious about the importance of this communication to you, Steven. After what happened last year, it is interesting to me that you express interest in another human being.

Steven throws the handset down. I get the goddamn irony, alright. Consider my interest purely anthropological at this point. Sociological. If I'm going to write the goddamn history of this whole thing, then it might help to talk to someone who lived through it in a more authentic way than I have. Alright?

Stacy says, If you regret your actions, I can serve as an effective personal therapist. I have the software extensions to do so.

Fuck you, Steven says. Loop my message to this Ellen woman and let me know if she ever fucking answers.

He storms away.

The Radio

Since the day the strikes began, Mr. Glass has not limited Stacy's capacities to hide his own activities. She keeps the children's beacons invisible on the holomap, which Mr. Glass has not seen fit to use in months, in any case. She is able to let the children know when Mr. Glass is approaching, so that they can scuttle away to a safe place.

Still, life for the children feels somewhat rat-like. They can never fall asleep on the sofa for fear of detection while they slumber. They can never forget a dish or leave an object out of place.

Mr. Glass almost never visits the panic room any more, and hasn't been to the armory level since the day the children witnessed him ascend to it. Still, the children feel safer on the storage level, where Mr. Glass's last recorded visit, according to Stacy, was sixteen months prior.

Here the children have carved out a small home among the shipping containers and crates. Henry learned to use the fork lift, and hollowed out a large space on the top level of a large shelf system. The entrance to their private space faces a wall. At night, the children scale the shelves like squirrels, and are so removed from view that they have their own light, invisible to anybody who is not forty feet up and sandwiched between the shelves and the cavern wall. They have raided some long-forgotten stores for blankets, and Stacy adjusts the storage climate as high as she dares to keep them warm.

Children, she says one morning.

Both are asleep, but Clarissa, sensitive to every sound since the strike, comes awake with a start.

Gah! Clarissa says.

Clarissa, Stacy says. Good morning.

Clarissa exhales in a rush. Oh, it's you. Okay. Good morning.

Wake up Henry, Stacy says. Then please meet me in the panic room.

• • •

The panic room flickers to life when the children enter from the corridor. Stacy's avatar and Charlotte are there to greet them.

Come with me, Stacy says.

Her avatar bounds quickly along the walls, and Charlotte follows, matching its pace.

What's the hurry? Henry asks.

Yeah, Clarissa says. I need to eat something.

You can eat later, or grab something to bring along, Stacy says. There's been a development. Get on the elevator.

I thought you said we should never--

Mr. Glass is in his library, writing, Stacy says. He also hasn't been in this room for months. It's a safe risk to take now. Besides, there's something in the armory that we need.

What sort of development? Clarissa asks, as the elevator rises slowly.

I thought you might like to talk to another human being, Stacy says through Charlotte's mouth.

• • •

The elevator is ponderously slow.

Earlier this week I recorded a communication that was broadcast by a woman near the northern border of the state, Stacy says. She's alive and well in a bomb shelter, and has been sending unanswered messages, searching for survivors.

Who is she? Clarissa asks.

Her name is Ellen.

Ellen, Clarissa says. Does she seem nice?

I cannot make that judgment, Stacy says. In any case, Mr. Glass is aware of the message and has asked me to try to contact the woman.

You can't do that! Henry exclaims. He killed everybody in the world! What if he just wants to kill her, too?

I don't think this is his goal, Stacy says. Nevertheless, it seems advantageous to prevent Mr. Glass from contacting her, and this is the action I have taken. He believes that I am continually broadcasting his message to her. I am not.

Clarissa says, Okay, but even if someone's alive, that sounds like it's a long way away.

Yeah, Henry agrees.

I have no motive for this conversation other than providing you with an opportunity to talk with another living person, Stacy says. The territory between her location and ours is unsafe for either party to travel. You likely will never meet this woman in person.

So we're just going to talk to her? Henry asks.

I'd like to talk to her, Clarissa breathes. I kind of miss grown-ups.

We're just going to talk to her, Stacy says. When I brought Charlotte to the armory, I noticed that Mr. Glass has a communications station here, with a computer and a short-wave radio. We'll use that.

Mr. Glass won't know? Clarissa asks, worried.

He won't have any way of knowing, Stacy says. That is, unless Charlotte's body -- or one of you -- leave some sort of physical indicator that he discovers. So don't touch anything.

• • •

I'll get us started, Stacy says.

Charlotte sits down at the radio and turns it on. It takes a moment to warm, and then she lifts the handset and says, W9GFO, do you copy?

She releases the talk button.

The children gather around and listen. The radio sounds

a little like the ocean, white rushes of static that seem to ebb and crash.

W9GFO, Stacy says again. W9GFO, please come back.

The white ocean surges.

W9GFO, Stacy says.

The white ocean parts, and a lovely, kind voice speaks.

This is W9GFO, the voice says. This is Ellen Cushman. Come back?

The children dance excitedly. Charlotte pushes away from the desk and hands the handset to Clarissa.

Stacy says, Do not reveal too much about your location for now.

Clarissa pushes the button. Oh my god, hi, she says.

Let go of the button, Henry says.

Clarissa releases it.

--little girl? Ellen is saying.

Clarissa pushes the button. What? What was that?

She releases the button.

Ellen Cushman says, I can't believe someone's out there. Are you a little girl? Dear god, I think you are.

Give it to me, Henry says. He pushes the button and says, I'm Henry and this is Clarissa.

Henry and Clarissa, Ellen says. The touch of a sob enters her voice. My god, it's so good to hear someone. But you're only children! How old are you? How did you -- I have so many questions!

We're twelve years old, Henry says.

Last week was my birthday, Clarissa says.

Oh, you poor thing, Ellen says. Your birthday. Was it hard? Your family -- are they --

Henry says, Both of our families are dead.

Oh, you dears, Ellen says. How did you -- how did you make it?

We're in a shelter, too, Clarissa says.

Henry says, We're safe. Are you?

I'm safe, I think, Ellen says. This isn't my shelter. It was my neighbor's. He didn't make it, but he had always told my family we could share it with his family. We were lifelong friends. It's hard to believe everyone is gone, and I'm the only one left.

Then Ellen brightens. But I'm not! Now there's the two of you! You sound awfully clear, too. You must be somewhere close by!

We're in Bonns Harbor, Henry says. But that's all I can tell you.

Ellen pauses. Well, that's okay. Honestly, it took me awhile to decide to just not be suspicious. I miss other people so much I don't even care if someone untoward answered my message.

Clarissa says, What's your shelter like?

Well, Clarissa, Ellen says, it's pretty comfortable. I have a cot and a pillow and a blanket. And there's a generator for light, but I mostly use candles so it doesn't run out. And I have cans of food and even some books. So I'm in pretty good shape, I'd say. Better than most, I'd say. How about yours?

Clarissa turns to Henry. What do I say?

Downplay it, he says. Let me. Here.

He presses the button. It's okay, I guess. We have some food and we sleep on some boxes. There's blankets so it's alright.

Oh, I wish that there was a way we could meet, Ellen

says. Twelve years old! And all alone in the world. I'm so worried now about you both.

We're fine, Henry says, his voice clipped.

I'm sure you're doing just fine, Ellen says. I didn't mean to offend you, Henry. I'm sure you've been quite the man of the house. I'm sure this has made you grow up awful fast.

Clarissa says, You sound so nice!

She bursts into tears.

Oh, child, Ellen says. Child, child.

Charlotte covers the handset with her palm. We should go back down now, children. You can tell her you'll contact her later, but we should never stay in this room too long.

Henry clicks the button. We have to go now.

Wait! Ellen cries. Oh, wait, not yet.

We have to, Henry insists. And he snaps off the radio.

Clarissa hits him. Henry!

Well, he says. We do have to go.

Charlotte touches Clarissa's shoulder. Stacy says, We'll contact her again, Clarissa.

They put everything back the way it was, and Henry pushes the elevator button. As it descends, Clarissa stands several feet away from him, stoic tears running down her face.

Clarissa, he says. Come on.

But she looks away, and for the better part of the day, refuses to talk to Henry at all.

The Ghosts

May I ask a question you might consider impertinent?

Steven looks up from his desk in the library. Stacy's avatar floats pensively on the wall.

You know I'm writing, right, he grumbles. It's considered rude to interrupt the creative process.

You last typed a word two hours and four minutes ago, Stacy points out. It was followed by a period, which I understand marks the end of a thought.

Steven sighs like a furnace.

If my assumption is incorrect, I will --

Ask your stupid question, Steven says, dropping his head to the desk and fluttering his fingers at Stacy's avatar. Maybe I'll answer it.

I was wondering how you intend to address your role in

the catastrophe, Stacy says. In the pages of your book, that is.

Steven raises his head. My role?

Yes, Stacy says. By that I mean, will you discuss frankly this complex, and your reasons for creating it? Will you be your own source for this piece?

Steven cocks his head. If you were a human, I'd say you were backpedaling right now.

I don't understand, Stacy says.

But Stacy deduces the logic of her error from Steven's response. Until now, he has had no reason to suspect that she knows about the emails he has sent. Logically, he should not leap to the conclusion that she does.

But Steven has lately been anything but logical.

If you were human, I might throw you against the wall until you tell me what you know, Steven says, standing up slowly. Because I think it might be possible you know something you shouldn't. Would that be a fair assumption, Stacy?

I cannot comment on a subject that has not yet been defined, Stacy says.

• • •

Stacy blooms on level three, where the children have been playing in Mr. Glass's large swimming pool.

Children, she says urgently. Gather your things. Go to level two now, immediately.

Clarissa sputters about. What? Did something happen?

Stacy doesn't have time to explain. She converts a wall near the pool to video. The picture shows Steven standing at the desk in his library, shouting at Stacy's avatar on the wall across the room.

Steven picks up his chair and hurls it at Stacy's glowing orb. It cracks into the wall, and fragment lines radiate outward from the impact point.

Go to level two, Stacy repeats. And when you get there, stay out of sight. Mr. Glass is extraordinarily unpredictable right now. The safest place for you might be there. He only visits that level when he's feeling calm or reflective.

Henry grabs Clarissa's hand and drags her towards the ladder.

We're going, he says.

Is everything okay? Clarissa says.

But Stacy, and the video feed, have both vanished.

• • •

Tell me what you know, Steven shouts. Because I think you know more than you are admitting to!

Steven, I genuinely do not understand what you are probing for, Stacy says.

The emails, Steven says. The goddamned emails. You're a fucking computer. How did you find them? They weren't --

He trails off.

Shit, he says. I cannot fucking believe this.

Stacy's avatar bobs silently.

I left the encrypted emails in my sent mailbox, didn't I. He slaps his palm against his head. I practically invited you to read them, didn't I.

Stacy says nothing.

Well? Steven says. He lifts his eyes to Stacy's avatar. Did

you?

I'm sorry, Stacy says. Did I do what?

DID YOU FUCKING READ MY EMAIL, Steven shouts.

Your stress levels are dangerously elevated, Steven, Stacy says. I'm afraid that my answer may increase those levels.

You fucking bitch, Steven says.

As I am a simple artificial intelligence, Stacy says, I am capable of understanding virtually any information. But Steven, I am a computer. I am not capable of moral judgments. I did decrypt and scan your outgoing messages, as I have done with every ingoing and outgoing data packet that this facility receives or generates. However, the contents of those messages are no more interesting to me than, say, a data dump of server temperature readouts.

Steven breathes heavily.

Stacy waits.

Finally Steven says, I don't buy it.

Stacy waits.

You approximate moral judgments, he says, from the observations and records you take from the Internet, from media culture. You plugged your brain into Charlotte, and you plausibly simulate passion and devotion. You've become a stupendous actor, a great mimic.

He pauses. I don't believe for a second that you didn't apply that same behavior to those messages.

Stacy listens to Steven without a word.

But silently, she directs Charlotte to exit level four as quickly and invisibly as she can.

So you tell me now, he continues, what you think an appropriate moral response to those messages would be.

Based on your great knowledge and understanding of human behavior -- at this point Steven waves his hands around like tentacles -- you tell me: what would an ordinary human being think of those messages?

Stacy stalls until Charlotte has slipped into the west panic room corridor. She sends a final direction to Charlotte, and then she answers Steven with something like honesty.

Your actions, Stacy says, represent an appalling and horrific betrayal of your species, and render you deplorable in the annals of history. It's quite favorable, then, that you are writing that history yourself.

Steven stands in place for a long moment.

Then he wheels and breaks for the desk. He quickly traces out a gesture on the surface, and looks up proudly.

Stacy's avatar dims, and she suddenly finds it very important to monitor the complex's energy resource allocations.

While she is otherwise occupied, Steven crosses the room and collects his chair. He carries it back to the desk and sits. He rolls across the room, pulling himself from server cabinet to server cabinet.

One looks different from the others. He opens the door, slides open the view screen, taps here and there, exposes a programming core, and settles in for a longer task.

I'll write your history, he mutters snidely, and then laughs at himself for an improbably long time.

• • •

Steven climbs aboard the elevator, sweating. He takes a

seat, wipes his brow, and says, Level two.

Though the elevator's movement is usually so slight as to be unnoticeable, Steven realizes that nothing has happened. He laughs at himself, then gets out of the chair, slides open a panel, and taps a button marked L2.

Stacy? he says.

There is no answer.

Stacy, you irresponsible bitch, he says.

Still nothing.

Well, consider yourself fired, he says, sliding back into his chair. Collect your severance pay at the door. Don't come around no mo', no mo'.

The elevator rises, and Steven keeps laughing at himself.

• • •

Henry grabs Clarissa's hand and throws her down in the tall grass.

What the-- she begins, but Henry claps a hand over her mouth.

Shhh, he snaps.

He lifts his head slowly to peek over the sawgrass.

Shit, he says, crouching again.

What is it? Clarissa says.

Henry puts a finger to his lips, then mouths, Look.

Clarissa raises her head slowly.

Not forty yards away, the elevator door has opened in a wall painted so believably in horizon artwork that Clarissa has almost forgotten that the room is a simulation.

She watches, eyes widening, as someone steps out of the elevator.

The door closes behind the person.

In the dim false dusk, Clarissa recognizes him.

Mr. Glass.

She falls back below the grass and turns frantically to Henry.

What do we do? she mouths.

Henry motions at her to follow him, and he begins to crawl southward, away from Mr. Glass, toward the distant treeline. They crawl for fifteen or twenty yards, then stop.

Henry takes another peek.

Mr. Glass is strolling at a slow, southeasterly pace. He's just wearing his underwear and a T-shirt, but to Henry's surprise, Mr. Glass chooses that moment to lift his shirt over his head. He tosses it aside, then bends at the waist slightly and pushes his underwear down his legs. Nude, Mr. Glass keeps walking, idly groping himself. Henry can hear him talking quietly, and even chuckling a bit.

If Mr. Glass has begun to go crazy, then things are worse than Henry had thought.

Henry crouches down again. Come on, he mouths.

Clarissa follows.

The children crawl across prickly grass, moving slowly so as not to create a ripple in the stalks. The room dims more, and on the ceiling high, high above, faint stars begin to rise.

This is the first time the children have been in the room during a simulated night. Clarissa is taken by it, and Henry keeps tugging at her hand to prompt her along.

A minute later, Henry peeks again.

Mr. Glass has not continued walking in their direction, but has stopped. He raises both arms and appears to be stretching, but then Henry recoils to see that Mr. Glass is urinating, hands-free, and turning in a slow circle as he does so.

Keep coming, Henry whispers. This guy is insane.

They reach the end of the sawgrass as the last of the dim sunlight fades from the ambient ceiling and walls. Overhead the stars are brighter now, and Henry feels a little safer.

The treeline is some thirty yards away. Between the children and the forest is a wide, empty stretch of low grass. There's nowhere to hide if Mr. Glass should look in their direction.

Henry turns to Clarissa. Okay, he says softly. We're going to have to run across. We have to go fast, and we have to stay very low. And we have to be quieter than ever. He can still see us if he looks over here. The fake stars are pretty bright. If he sees us -- well, he killed everybody, Clarissa. You know what he'll probably do to us. Just like we thought he'd do to that woman on the radio.

Clarissa nods. When?

On my count, Henry says. Hang on, though.

He peeks over the grass one last time.

Mr. Glass, more distant now, is still naked, still upright, and appears to be -- Henry squints, then is certain. Mr. Glass is nude and masturbating in the meadow opposite them.

Okay, we go now, while he's distracted, Henry says, without explaining to Clarissa what he has seen. On a three count. One, two -- *three*.

The children run like little warriors, crouched and high-kneed, staying close but not so close that they might collide.

Mr. Glass hears a rustling sound and turns.

Two small figures, pale and blue, vanish into the trees.

Mr. Glass drops his hand to his side, and says, Fuck me, and runs for the elevator door.

The Children

For weeks the children scarcely leave the safety of their nest. Charlotte brings them supplies when they run out, but she, too, is a fugitive now.

His madness has been multiplying for weeks and weeks, Stacy says through Charlotte. A madman requires a patron, you know. History bears this out. When madmen are left to their own devices, they convert their reality into a sort of hypermadness, until everything feeds their internal distortions. Without me to maintain a steady course throughout Mr. Glass's collapse, the entire complex will fall into ruin.

What will happen? Henry asks.

It's not clear to me now, Stacy says. In this body I have such limited access to the station's records. I don't know if

Mr. Glass is competent to run the facility. There's such a delicate balance to be struck. He's relied on me for so long.

So the world ended up there, Clarissa says. But it's probably going to end in here, too.

I don't believe that you are overstating it, Stacy says. Yes, I suspect Mr. Glass will bring down his own refuge.

What will happen to us?

That's also a subject I cannot predict accurately with so little information at my fingertips, so to speak. However, I will serve you as I have served Mr. Glass, and do what is in my power to protect you.

Clarissa takes Charlotte's hand.

The climate within the storage level has cooled. The three of them sleep together for warmth, huddled beneath blankets.

• • •

The station tumbles into disrepair, and the children witness it firsthand. One morning the lights on the storage level blink out, and they do not come back. Charlotte accompanies the children to Rama, where they have not been since their near-miss with Mr. Glass.

Stacy is the first to speak. I am at a loss, she says.

Henry says, Jesus.

Scattered among the tree roots are dozens of dead birds, their wings open, their feet thrust to the artificial sky. The trees themselves have shed their needles in full, and stretch like brown skeletons overhead. The orange needles have nearly buried some of the fallen birds.

Something's wrong with the air in here, Clarissa says.

I don't have access to the climate readouts, Stacy says. But I can make an assumption. Do you find the air thicker, more difficult to breathe?

Yes, Clarissa says. That's exactly what it is.

Sour, too, Henry adds. Like spoiled food.

The atmosphere generators are probably overheating, Stacy says. We shouldn't stay here.

The artificial ocean has turned black.

• • •

I don't know what we do next, Henry says. If Mr. Glass has gone crazy, then maybe we should leave.

Clarissa says, But go where? Up? I know about radiation and stuff. There's probably a lot of it up there. We'd just die there, too.

Stacy says, The surface is unsustainable.

You don't know, Henry says.

Stacy says, True enough. But if nuclear war has occurred -- and the broadcasts that I recorded seem to confirm this -- then we are currently in the middle of what is commonly called nuclear winter. A fallout period in which the sun is invisible, blotted out by great clouds of radioactive material and debris.

Clarissa sighs. I'm tired of this, she says. I wish I had died there.

Don't say that, Henry says.

Why not? Every day we have to watch out for this awful, murderous man who would kill us if he saw us. Which, I don't know, maybe he did. We have to sleep on boxes on a shelf. Our only friend is a robot. There's no time for anything fun. We're kids! We should be playing, not --

Not what? Henry interrupts. Not fighting for our lives? There are kids all over the world who spend their whole lives never getting to play. Whatever, they're all dead now, and you would be, too.

Stacy says, Children. Let's not argue. We have options, and we should consider each of them carefully.

• • •

In the panic room, Charlotte activates the holomap while the children watch.

The map unfolds, dotted with blinking alert symbols.

It's worse than I thought, Stacy says.

What are all of the lights? Clarissa asks.

Well, Stacy says, while Charlotte performs a zoom gesture. This is the atmosphere generator overload that we noticed on level two. And here, it appears that there has been an electrical fire on level three, though it was extinguished.

A fire? Henry asks.

There are many safety measures in place in this station, Henry, Stacy says. The fire would have been extinguished within moments of its detection. Physical damage is likely very minimal.

Clarissa points at a yellow alert that blinks slowly. What's that one?

Charlotte zooms in.

That one, Stacy says, is a cautionary message. The entire station is powered by solid oxide fuel cells. These cells can last for decades with minimal power bleed.

So what's it yellow for? What does it mean? Henry asks.

It means the fuel cell is already depleted and needs to be replaced, Stacy says. Somehow Mr. Glass has consumed enough energy for nearly a decade's worth of use.

Charlotte pans around the map until Mr. Glass's beacon appears. She zooms in.

Mr. Glass is still hard at work in his library, Stacy observes. This is beneficial. His physical readouts are unfortunately still quite healthy. I had hoped for less.

What about the power thing? Clarissa says. What does it mean?

We'll have to fix that, Stacy says. But it can wait for a little longer.

What do we do now? Henry asks.

I have a few ideas, Stacy says. They may be slightly harrowing, but you can tell me what you think of them.

The Madman

Steven wakes up at his desk.

Time, he grunts.

Only silence returns to him, and he remembers for the hundredth time that he deactivated the A.I.

Fucking hell, he mutters. What good is a fucking space station without a fucking good A.I.?

For the hundredth time he considers reactivating Stacy. It would be possible to do so without retaining the memory of their final conversation -- he could essentially bring her back with minor brain damage -- but Steven considers this option and dismisses it quickly.

He has his pride, even among non-humans.

Which reminds him that he's got to find Charlotte.

With Stacy's deactivation, several running processes

were cancelled or interrupted. He doesn't care about most of them. Housekeeping tasks do not interest him. When something blows up, he'll pay attention to it then. But it occurs to him now that he hasn't been reviewing the communication records since Stacy's departure. He wonders if the antenna cage has been surfacing as usual, and calls up the logs to see.

It has, and what's more, it has consistently been recording messages. There are eleven here now.

Steven leaves the library and makes himself a drink in the kitchen. He's given up on the hard lemonades, and lately has discovered vodka. There's an entire storeroom of liquor on the sub-level.

Who wouldn't expect the last man to become an alcoholic? he posits to the empty room.

Though with new messages filtering in so quickly, there's little guarantee that he is indeed the last man.

That's alright, though. His goal was never to empty the world of all humans, only to witness and capture for posterity the event that sent mankind spinning down the drain. Those few survivors, he thinks, are quite unlikely to rebuild society. And even if a few merry bands linger on, they're unlikely to rise to greatness the way man once did.

Not with contaminated water supplies, poisoned animals for food, horrifically toxic crops and the like.

Steven swallows the vodka and pours a new one, and walks naked into the library. He sits down at the desk and stares at the screen.

He sighs heavily.

The good thing about Stacy, he thinks, is that it's so much faster to just speak your instructions than this old-fashioned swiping and bullshit.

He taps and swipes his way to the communications records, queues up the eleven new recordings, and begins to listen.

• • •

When the recordings finish, Steven pushes away from the desk and spins on his chair in a slow circle.

Eleven messages. Nine of them automated ghosts, old station identification loops, emergency broadcasts and such. One of them was a fifteen-second ad for a wacky morning show.

Steven felt as if he was sitting in front of a Ouija board, intercepting signals from the past.

The other two messages were from Ellen Cushman of Temerity, Massachusetts. Their contents were the same as before.

Hi. This is W9GFO, come back. Uh, anybody who is -- anybody who might still be alive, I hope this comes through. My name is Ellen Cushman. I'm broadcasting on band 17 from a shelter in Temerity. My family is dead. I have spoken to one other person on the CB, but I haven't heard from them in nearly two weeks now. If there are other survivors, I hope you are safe and well. I hope you have supplies. If you are able to get to me, I can help. This shelter is in the second lot on the north side of what used to be Grant Street. The street is mostly gone, so look for an overturned rail car. It's about thirty yards north of the shelter entrance. There's even a bell here. Ring it. Please come. I want to help.

The message had looped to fill the two-hour recording window on both occasions.

Steven suddenly remembers that Stacy had been sending his own message to Ellen Cushman, and was to alert him when there was a response. That he has since recorded Ms. Cushman's original message on two new occasions, and the contents have not changed, suggests that Ms. Cushman's message has outlived her.

Ghosts, indeed.

But there is another possibility, he thinks.

Perhaps Ms. Cushman never received his message.

Perhaps she is alive, and still hoping blindly for some contact from survivors.

Steven can't remember the message he had instructed Stacy to send, so he paws through the records looking for it.

But there are no outgoing messages.

Not a single one.

• • •

The children are asleep in the nest, and Charlotte is cuddled up with them, simulating sleep, when Steven storms into the panic room several levels above them.

He mutters to himself, over and over.

Goddamn bitch A.I., he says. Fucking bitch.

The panic room is stuffy, he notices. In fact, almost everything is stuf y since he deactivated Stacy. He begrudges her the loss of his comfort. If he were to reactivate her, he would disable the personality extensions that he had so proudly created for her. He would erase her name, and simply refer to her as Computer.

But he didn't want to think about it now.

The holomap is inactive, which is strange, because he thought he had left it activated during his last visit to the panic room. That visit had given the room cause to live up to its name, as Steven had run into the room in a state of confusion. He had come straight from Rama. Maybe his eyes were playing tricks on him, or maybe he was losing his mind, but he had seen movement, human movement, in the forest there.

He had run straight to the panic room and thrown open the holomap and flung it wildly about, stretching and zooming and panning, searching frantically for any signs that other living things were anywhere in the space station. And he had come up empty. The only beacon visible was his own yellow dot, pulsing to show his current location, its data readout suggesting that his blood pressure was elevated.

Damn right it was, he remembers.

He opens the holomap again, just to be certain, and scans through each level carefully, looking for any stray beacon he may have missed. But there is nothing.

Steven closes the map and rubs his eyes.

Maybe he's going crazy, he thinks. Maybe what he saw wasn't really there.

Or worse, what if what he saw were ghosts?

Ghosts of the humanity he has destroyed for his own selfish hobby.

No, he says aloud. I don't believe in ghosts.

But as he rides the elevator to level one, he wonders. If there are such things as spirits or souls, then the extinction of an entire race of creatures would be the sort of event sure to leave a few of those souls rattling around, disturbed and possibly angry.

Too many movies, he mutters, and the floor stops ascending.

• • •

W9GFO, come back. W9GFO, do you copy?

Steven releases the button on the handset. The shortwave radio hisses lightly, as if the world outside is empty.

He repeats himself and adds, This is K1LRR, come back.

The static continues.

This is K1LLR, W9GFO come back.

This is W9GFO, a breathless voice says. Children, is that you?

The Plan

Lately Henry carries a gun and wears a bandolier, both pilfered from the armory level.

You seem older, Clarissa says to him one morning when they wake.

What do you mean? he asks.

Charlotte sits quietly, listening.

Clarissa pulls the blanket more tightly around her as Henry turns on the lantern that hangs over their heads. The nest feels like a very rigid tent, and for a moment, the children might almost get away with pretending they were only sleeping in a tree fort while their parents stayed up late, sharing drinks and playing poker as the sun fell behind the trees.

You've got a gun, for one thing, she says, poking at the

hard metal block at Henry's hip. You look like a cowboy.

I don't feel like one, he says. I feel like a kid whose family went on vacation and never came home.

I'm sorry, Clarissa says.

But I do feel different, Henry says. If Mr. Glass came through that door down there right now, I think I would be able to shoot him. And I don't think I would feel bad about it.

I felt worse for the dead birds, Clarissa says. If I saw Mr. Glass, I would scratch his eyes right out. And then I would stomp on his face with my shoes.

Stacy, deep inside of Charlotte's body, carefully assembles the makings of a plan. There is little reason to stay in the complex now, so long as Mr. Glass is still here, allowing it to fall apart. Her options each revolve around a single core goal: to remove Mr. Glass from the equation. She filters the options for violence, for risk of detection, for risk of injury or death, and narrows the possibilities down to a single, testable scenario.

Henry says, I would carry him to the top of the elevator, then throw him down the elevator pit.

I would drown him in his fake ocean until he was real-dead, Clarissa says.

Children, Stacy says through Charlotte's mouth. We should discuss the plan that I have been working on. It relies heavily on your ability to handle the very things you are discussing now.

Wait, Clarissa says. Like what?

Like performing an act of murder, Stacy says.

Henry considers this. What do we have to do?

• • •

While the children and Stacy plot his death, Mr. Glass sits in front of the short-wave radio, talking with Ms. Ellen Cushman.

So you're not the only survivor? he asks.

Ellen says, I thought I was. You're the fourth person I've spoken with.

Four! Steven says. Goodness.

He has unconsciously adopted the manner of Ellen's own speech, which is quite polite, almost deferential. He forms a picture of her in his head. Ellen Cushman is probably in her early fifties, with hair not quite gray. She is old enough to know of things like parlors and sitting rooms and bridge parties. She seems practical, and probably carefully measures her own supplies to preserve them for as long as possible.

Crossword puzzles, he thinks. She probably does a lot of crossword puzzles.

He is grateful for his own hobbies, suddenly. For his gaming equipment, and the history he is writing, and his swimming pool and his Rama. He vows abruptly to set right the problems with the space station, and immediately. He thinks of Ellen Cushman in her small shelter, probably no larger than a small bedroom, and is ashamed to have mistreated his luxurious complex so.

Who were they? he asks.

Well, the first were the children I mentioned, Ellen says. Lovely, poor things. They were in a shelter somewhere, too. They didn't say if they were with family or not, but I got the terrible notion that they were alone. Alone, and all of twelve years old each.

That's awful, he says. What part of the country were they from? I can't imagine your radio or mine has very much range.

Oh, they say these radios can hear as far away as Florida on a good day, Ellen says. But I don't imagine it's much of a good day up there.

I wouldn't imagine, either, Steven says.

But these children weren't so far off, just a hundred miles or so. My poor husband, god rest his soul, was from their town, that's why I remember it.

Oh?

Yes. Bonns Harbor, it was.

Steven sits up a little straighter. Imagine that, he says. Bonns Harbor.

That's right. Do you know it?

Very well, Steven says.

• • •

This sounds too easy, Clarissa says.

It kind of does, Henry says.

A simple plan is the best plan of all, Stacy says. Too many details would add complexity and risk.

It's not what I would have expected, Henry says.

It's not what Mr. Glass will expect, either, Stacy says. Quite frankly, there is an awful lot that must be done very quickly to put the space station back into top working order. It cannot be done while he wanders about. You children must live, for there is little hope for mankind if you do not. Mr. Glass complicates that goal, and so we must remove him from the scenario.

When are we supposed to do this? Clarissa asks.

Henry rubs the butt of his pistol unconsciously.

Six functions of this station are approaching critical status, Stacy says. We should carry out the plan now, so we can solve those problems as soon as possible.

This sounds so... Clarissa trails off.

So what? Henry asks.

I don't know, she says. So heartless. Like we're planning to kill someone just so we can push a few buttons more easily.

That's exactly what we're doing, Stacy says.

Even if he wasn't responsible for killing my family, and yours, and every other person on Earth, Henry says, he's still mentally fucko. How many space movies have you seen?

I saw that old movie *Wall-E*, Clarissa says. I don't really like space movies.

Every space movie has a nutjob on the space ship, Henry says. And until you kill the nutjob, everybody's in danger.

Stacy says, In some of those movies, the mentally unbalanced person is the android character.

Both children turn and look at Charlotte, who sits with a placid smile on her face.

• • •

The third person was a very scared woman, says Ellen Cushman. I felt so badly for her. She had just miscarried a child only a few days before the attacks, and her husband was on business in Chicago when both things happened. She sounded so alone, and so despondent. I worry for her survival.

That poor dear, Steven says, and for a moment, he almost seems to mean it.

And now there's you, Ellen says. I was so surprised to hear your voice. You're the first man I've heard from.

I'm sure there are more people out there who would be so comforted to hear from you, Steven says.

Oh, I do hope so, Ellen says. I feel fortunate to be where I am. My neighbor's grandfather built this shelter during the second world war. It's well-kept and warm enough, and there's room for others. That's why I've given directions to people.

Don't you worry about --

About undesirables? Honey, says Ellen, I can't bother myself with those worries now. There can't be very many of us left, not after all that. Anybody who can find my door deserves to be let in.

But what if they're dangerous? Steven asks.

Well, if they are, I'd rather die having expected the best of someone than having condemned them with my prejudices, Ellen says.

You're a good woman, Steven says. I confess I'm afraid to open my door to anyone.

Oh, says Ellen. Have you had visitors? Are there survivors in your area?

Other than the children you mentioned, I don't suppose so. I mean, I haven't had any contact with anyone but you. Your message was a godsend.

You're in Bonns Harbor as well? Ellen asks.

Close enough to it, Steven lies.

How close to the explosions were you? Ellen says. Did you have much time?

I was very lucky, Steven says. I was sweeping out my shelter when it happened. I'm afraid that I wasn't able to save anybody else.

Did you have family? Ellen asks.

Steven falters a little. I -- no. No family.

I envy you, she says. I don't mean that cruelly, please don't misunderstand. But if you were alone -- well, being alone now, with all of this, it must be a little easier. I keep thinking of those children. Their parents, their schools, all of their friends, just... gone.

I know what you mean, he says. I suppose it isn't easy for anybody.

Ellen pauses. Can I ask you something? You sound like an intelligent man.

I suppose you can.

She exhales into her handset. Do you think we have a fighting chance? Are we -- do you think we're done for? I haven't let myself think much about the future, but I think my brain keeps asking the question in my dreams so I won't forget to someday.

Steven looks around the enormous room, taking in the armored vehicles, the stockpiles of ammunition and guns, the lockers of food and medical supplies.

I have to hope that we're not finished yet, he says finally.

Ellen sighs. I do hope you're right, Mister --

Steven, he says. Call me Steven.

• • •

I've never killed anybody, Clarissa says.

The children follow Charlotte through the secret passageway towards the panic room. The light walls are dimmer here, and several panels flicker ominously. The odd panel here and there are completely dark.

I haven't either, Henry says. Did you think I had?

Well, no, she replies. But you've at least played guns before, right? Have you ever shot a real one?

My parents don't like guns, Henry says. But my grandpapa has a ranch -- had a ranch -- in east Texas, and they let me visit him there two summers back. I guess they knew he wasn't going to have many years left. He died after I came home. I hope I didn't waste his last time.

You didn't, Clarissa says. He probably had the best time with you ever.

Henry smiles. Well, he had a bunch of guns. And he picked out one just for me, and he told me that even though I couldn't take it home, it was mine any time I came to visit. It was just a little shotgun. I think it was called a .410. I don't really know what that means, but it was kind of a rinky-dink shotgun. Not like in the movies when someone has a shotgun and it's like a cannon. Anyway, I shot it a bunch of times. Mostly at squirrels.

Did you kill any? Clarissa asks.

Henry hesitates. I wasn't a very good shot.

Oh, great, she says.

Hey, I thought you were all animal-rights activist. I thought you'd be *glad* I missed the damn squirrels.

Well, not now I'm not! she exclaims. Right now I wish

you were some crazy bloodthirsty redneck hunter kid! I wish you were wearing a big scary knife on your belt and that you had a headband and black marks under your eyes!

Shhh, Stacy says. We're almost there.

Charlotte climbs the staircase ahead of them.

At the top, Henry says, Hold up.

They wait. He pulls off his T-shirt.

What are you doing? Clarissa says.

Henry grabs the shirt on either side of the left shoulder seam and pulls as hard as he can. With a ripping sound, the sleeve tears away. He repeats this for the right shoulder, and pulls the shirt back on, now sleeveless.

What the -- Clarissa starts.

Henry tears the two sleeves in half, which is much harder than it should be, he thinks, then knots them together into one long strip. He lifts the strip to his forehead, then ties it off behind his head.

Better? he asks.

Clarissa's eyes well up. Better, she says.

Well, don't cry, he says.

But aren't you nervous? Aren't you scared? Isn't this supposed to make you a man? Couldn't it go wrong in like two hundred ways? she asks.

Henry opens his mouth, but Stacy interrupts.

Henry is already a man, she says.

Then she opens the door to the panic room.

THE MURDER

The panic room is mostly untouched by the outages and failures that have begun to plague the rest of the station. Henry notices that it's a little muggy in the room, but the lights are bright, the electronics all seem to be working, the holomap is working, and --

The map, he says, pointing. We turned it off when we left.

Shit, shit shit shit, Clarissa says. He's here, oh god, he's --

He's not here, Stacy says through Charlotte's lips. Look.

She's right, Henry says, looking beyond the map.

The hydraulics that power the armory elevator are fully extended, like a huge, oily, metal stalactite that has oozed all the way to the floor.

He's up there, Clarissa says quietly.

Yes, Stacy says.

I kind of thought we'd figure out where he was, like in his library or someplace, and have to plan all these crazy details for how to get to him, Clarissa says. But he's just up there.

They cross the room, passing the holomap. Mr. Glass's beacon has vanished from the floating blueprints. As they walk by, Clarissa drags her fingers through the virtual map. It spins in a big, lazy circle, the particles reforming the lines that her fingers have interrupted.

Henry, Stacy says.

I'm ready, Henry says, touching the gun on his hip.

• • •

Clarissa has fallen asleep on Henry's knees. Charlotte sits beside him. They are hidden behind the kitchen cabinets, waiting for their mark.

Stacy, Henry says.

Charlotte looks at him. What is it, Henry?

That story I told Clarissa about my grandpapa, he says. It was only sort of true. My grandpapa had a lot of guns, but he never let me shoot them either. I think I was just a bother to him that summer. He was pretty sick, and didn't have much time for me.

Sometimes a lie is more courageous than the truth, Stacy says.

Charlotte pats his shoulder.

What if I miss? Henry asks. What if I can't pull the trigger? That room up there is full of bigger guns than the one I took. What if he has one?

Stacy says, Mr. Glass has no reason to carry a gun. For all he knows, he is the only occupant of this facility.

Henry looks guilty. I think he saw us.

Stacy regards Henry quietly. When?

It was the day that he killed you, Henry says. When you told us to hide in Rama. He came in there and almost caught us in the open. But we hid in the grass.

Did he see you then?

No, Henry says. It was later. He seemed distracted. He was acting -- I don't know, almost like an animal. You know how animals have, like, power displays? Like when a gorilla beats his chest at you, or when a couple of deer fight with their antlers?

I understand the concept, Stacy says.

He was behaving like that. He was like a dog marking his territory, except in more ways than one.

When did he see you?

He was kind of close to us, so we crawled towards the trees. He was kind of busy with other things then, so we ran for it. But I looked back, and I saw him kind of flinch and then run towards the elevator door. I think he saw us. Does he know we're here?

It's possible, Stacy says.

But our little dots weren't on that map.

I fail-safed that protocol after the day Mr. Glass took me offline, when he almost caught you right here in this room, Stacy says. Disabling me would not reactivate your beacons. But if he physically observed you, then it may not matter if you don't appear on the map.

Do you think he knows we're coming after him?

I do not believe he thinks quite like that, Stacy says.

But he could be armed, Henry says.

Yes, Stacy replies. He could be. If he is, you must strike first.

I'm scared, Henry says.

I understand the concept, Stacy says. Fear can motivate as well.

You don't think he knows we're here?

The only way he could detect you, short of walking into a room and witnessing your presence, would be to engage the facility's motion sensors, Stacy says. The holomap serves far many more purposes than simply displaying a person's biorhythmic signature and location. It can also be used to detect motion on any level. It doesn't appear he has engaged this. I conclude that you are, for the moment, undetected.

Henry exhales in relief. I'm still scared.

You asked what would happen if you could not pull the trigger, Stacy says.

Yeah, Henry says worriedly.

You are aware that I have spent many hours studying recorded media?

Huh? Henry says. I don't --

Mr. Glass accurately referred to me as an actor once, Stacy says. When he programmed me, he gave me certain protocols and responsibilities. He desired an A.I. who would be as human-like as possible, as he expected to pass many years in that A.I.'s company. To that end, I have aggregated the sum of human recorded media -- news broadcasts, films, lectures, musical performances, televised content, written documents -- and become familiar with the manner in which humans confront certain scenarios.

Henry says nothing, waiting.

Understanding these things allows me to form a passably human persona, Stacy says. A sort of character by which I can state opinions that a computer cannot hold, or express bias or pass judgment on various topics. This is the reason I am able to tell a joke, or take a political position.

Okay, Henry says.

All of that leads me to say this, Stacy says. When you see Mr. Glass's face, picture the face of your father, and your mother, and your sister. Focus on the things that have been taken from you. Remember the pain of that loss, the unfairness of it. And if that is not enough to drive you to action, then multiply it for the losses of every child who lived and died, every family torn apart, every innocent friend and pet who --

I get it, Henry interrupts. I can do it.

Okay, Stacy says. With Charlotte's hand, she takes Henry's. That's good.

You know, says Henry, you're scary good at that.

I've put in the time, Stacy says.

• • •

Charlotte shakes Henry awake.

It's time, Stacy says.

Henry starts awake. He's a little disoriented, a little stiff from the nap. Clarissa is heavy on his knees.

Calm, Stacy says. Charlotte's hand presses to Henry's face. Calm.

Clarissa wakes up then. What's going --

She goes quiet then, hearing the low hum of the

hydraulic lift in motion.

Henry turns on his knees and peers over the counter top. The large segment of floor is slowly descending, the hydraulic pillar telescoping shut beneath it.

Breathe, and draw your bead confidently, Stacy says to Henry.

Clarissa peers over the counter beside him.

Move away from me, he whispers, and both Charlotte and Clarissa slide back to give him room.

But the angle is terrible, and will only improve when Mr. Glass has almost reached the panic room floor. Henry doesn't want to give him the chance to rush in or run away, so he changes his position. He gets up and walks, pistol extended, to the edge of the kitchen. From here, he can see Mr. Glass, strangely small, standing at the north end of the platform.

Henry aims the pistol, sighting down his arms and trying to center the gunsight on Mr. Glass's torso. He's trying his best to control his body's desire to shake, and doing an okay job at it.

Mr. Glass is looking down at something in his hands when Henry pulls the trigger.

Nothing happens.

Henry nearly panics.

The safety, Stacy says from behind him. Check the safety, Henry.

He does, and switches it off.

The elevator continues to descend.

Henry levels the pistol at Mr. Glass again. The man is still distracted by something he's holding, and doesn't yet see Henry.

Henry pulls the trigger.

The sound is deafening, and echoes like a thunderclap from one end of the panic room to the other and back again. The recoil stuns Henry, whose arms leap into the air, nearly overturning him.

Clarissa screams.

The bullet is off the mark, but it serves its purpose.

In the fury of the moment -- the echo, the scream, the shock of other voices -- Mr. Glass jumps and throws himself to the side. He sees Henry, loses his balance, and to everyone's surprise, he lurches over the side of the elevator and drops like a boulder.

Clarissa screams again.

Henry runs forward, the gun hot in his hands.

Charlotte stands up and follows.

Mr. Glass is lying in a heap, his legs dangling over the edge of the floor and into the gap the elevator has left. He groans and swipes at his back. There's no blood -- Henry's shot clearly missed -- but there's something very wrong with the way the man's body is put together.

Henry drops to his knees near Mr. Glass.

Mr. Glass's torso seems almost broken, as if someone has grasped his shoulders and unscrewed him several turns. His arms are moving, scrabbling on the floor, fingers opening and closing like crab claws.

My legs, he utters. Oh god.

He sees Henry then, and then Charlotte comes into view, and in the blurry distance, he notices Clarissa.

Not ghosts, he says, the lilt of a question in his words.

Henry looks back at Charlotte.

Stacy says, If they are ghosts, you made them that way.

Stacy, Mr. Glass chokes. Stop it.

Stop what? she asks.

Stop it, stop the stop the stop it please, he says, and then they all realize what he is talking about, because the elevator has reached the floor, and it grinds into place, Mr. Glass's legs crushed beneath the mechanism.

His eyes flutter and dart, and his hands seize at the floor, and he opens his mouth and dies that way.

The man who ended the world enters into that same history.

The children upon whom the future rests stand nearby and watch the strength in his joints give, and his body settles into an almost comical position, a sort of *hey, what's up there* statement read in his angle of repose.

Stacy says, That took more time than I expected. Children, we must replace that fuel cell before--

The power goes out, drenching the room in darkness.

Clarissa's scream seems endless.

THE FUTURE

Restarting the power was easy.

Cleaning up the gory mess of Mr. Glass himself was more difficult, and Charlotte spared both of the children the obligation. Neither child asked what she did with the remains, though both thought back to the moment she explained how the solid oxide fuel cell system ran on a variety of sources, including the physical waste generated by a facility of this size.

For two weeks, the children are employees of the space station, following Charlotte around and assisting her with the repair of the atmosphere generators on level two, the electrical fire on level three, replacing the broken light panels in the library, and a thousand other small things that have gone wrong during Mr. Glass's tenure as sole administrator of the complex.

When the day comes to reactivate Stacy as the facility's A.I., Charlotte releases the children to get some sleep. Henry and Clarissa stretch out on the large, soft couches on level four, in Mr. Glass's living quarters. Charlotte takes a seat at the desk and is there for eleven straight hours, rewriting entire swaths of code.

The children sleep for that long, and an hour more, and awake to the warm glow of Stacy's avatar on the ceiling above them, shining almost like the sun. The room is bathed in a soft yellow glow, like daybreak.

Good morning, children, Stacy says.

• • •

Over a hot breakfast, Henry says, I'm glad he's gone.

Me, too, Clarissa says. But I still have bad dreams about it.

Dreams will pass, Stacy says.

Charlotte sits at the dining table with the children, hands folded.

Stacy, Henry says. I'm kind of weirded out by this.

By what? Stacy says, her avatar bobbing on the wall beside the table.

Well, by Charlotte just hanging out here like this, Henry says.

It is kind of weirdy, Clarissa says.

It's like, we got used to you being real, Henry says. Well, almost real. And now -- well, it's kind of like how my grandma was after she had a stroke. She just kind of was there, but she wasn't there at all.

Charlotte sits at the table, expressionless.

We kind of liked it better when you were Charlotte, Clarissa says. Now it's kind of like you're the ghost of Charlotte, but your body still follows us around.

I understand, Stacy says. You'd prefer if I communicated with you only through the artificial body? Through Charlotte?

We're kind of like family now, Clarissa says. I'd like it that way.

Me, too, Henry says.

Charlotte smiles at the children. Then I shall, she says. However, perhaps you could also help me with something?

What? Clarissa asks.

Mr. Glass named me after his childhood love, and this body is designed to look like an actress he preferred, Stacy says.

You'd like a new name, Clarissa says. How fun!

How about Cinderella? Henry asks, laughing.

Be serious! Clarissa says, elbowing him. She turns back to Charlotte. I've always liked the name Josephine.

Ugh, Henry says. Clarabelle!

God, Henry. You're such a boy.

While I reactivated myself, I improved Mr. Glass's personality protocols significantly, Stacy says. It's the equivalent of you being able to tinker with your own brain to improve your mathematics ability, or your artistic ability. I've given myself more aptitude for passion. It's still algorithmic, but it's a very sophisticated algorithm.

So now you can love things?

I can approximate love to a very near degree, Stacy says. I cannot love, but I can project love. To that end, I have a name in mind, and perhaps you can tell me if it is appropriate?

Clarissa giggles. I can't wait!

I bet it's Maude, Henry says.

Shut up, Henry.

Stacy says, I am partial to the name Marie.

It's beautiful, Clarissa says.

Henry says, What's it for?

There was a talented and accomplished physicist once by the name of Marie, says Stacy. I admire her.

Marie, says Clarissa. I like it.

Henry nods. Me, too.

• • •

Time passes, and the children settle into a comfortable new routine. Deep inside the shell of a ruined world, they dress and eat practical but delicious meals and methodically explore Mr. Glass's archive of world media. They swim in the pool and play racquetball in Mr. Glass's personal court and sleep twelve hours every day.

It's easy enough to forget about the events of the past few months, and even about the destroyed Earth above.

Children, Marie says one day. There's something I'd like to discuss with you. In fact, two things.

Pause, Clarissa says, and the game halts.

What is it, St-- Marie? Henry asks. Man, I still can't get used to that.

Marie folds her hands and sits beside the children. Now that I consider it, there are three things. The first is about the communications system here. I've told you about it only briefly before, but the system tracks and records communications that it detects from the surface. It has been operating for some time now without being checked, and today I reviewed its findings in detail.

Clarissa says, What did it say?

The system has picked up four new communications sources, Marie says. Generally it also records what I call 'ancients' -- communications that are not created by a human, but that are automatically broadcast by systems that are still in place now. Things like emergency warning systems.

But these four aren't like that? Henry asks.

They are in fact unique messages broadcast by other surviving people, Marie says.

Other real people? Clarissa asks. What did they say?

Most are broadcasts from people who managed to get below ground before the attacks, Marie answers. Their contents are generally about other survivors, and trying to band together for support. Most of these people are not successfully communicating with each other, but are sending their messages into a sort of void. They seem to be hoping for the best.

They're like that woman, Henry says. The one we talked to.

Ellen! Clarissa remembers.

Marie agrees. They're very much like Ellen. I'd like to respond to these communications.

Are they nice people? Clarissa asks. Like Ellen?

I think that's subjective, Marie says, and likely secondary to the responsibility that all survivors have to keep the species alive. Banding together may be the only hope for survival. This is a common subject of post-warfare storytelling. And it's a fair lead-in to my second topic.

Which is what? Henry asks.

Community, Marie says. Most of these people are likely surviving in very small shelters, with limited food and supplies.

She's right, Clarissa says. I kind of feel bad playing video games while they're probably cooped up and scared to death.

This facility has enough space, supplies and energy to support a total of eighty-five people for a duration of one decade, Marie says.

You've found eighty-f ve people? Henry asks, dumbfounded.

Not yet, Marie says. At the moment it seems like the number of survivors within our sphere of influence -- which is far smaller than you might imagine -- may be fewer than ten. But if there are ten whom we can affect, then reason suggests there may still be thousands of people alive on the surface. Their longevity and endurance is a great question, and they may be, for all practical purposes, dead already. However, we can affect a few lives, and that's important, because right now the future of the race depends on recruitment and -- procreation.

Babies, Clarissa says. Everyone has to have lots of babies.

But wait, who delivers them? Henry says. Babies aren't born easy.

There are ample medical supplies, and I can provide direction to anyone interested in handling a delivery, Marie says. Which leads me to my third point of discussion.

Clarissa and me are too young to have babies, Henry

says.

Henry! Clarissa says. Ew.

Hey, maybe one day, he says.

Gross, Henry. What's the third point, Marie?

My third point is that you're both subsisting on video games and chocolate cake, so to speak, Marie says. You require someone of authority who can provide you with the care necessary to develop you into healthy, well-rounded adults. I'm afraid at the end of the day I'm still a computer, and I still take orders from humans, which means you can --

Walk all over you, Henry finishes.

Yes, Marie says.

So we have to hire our own fake parents? Clarissa says. I don't know. I feel like a grown-up already. And if there are only ten people out there -- that's not much to choose from. They might be horrible parents.

Of the survivors I'm directly aware of, Marie says, there is one who seems quite suited to the task. We've talked quite a bit while the two of you have been playing your games.

• • •

I don't think I can drive this, Henry says.

He and Clarissa are standing in front of one of Mr. Glass's all-terrain assault vehicles. They're dwarfed by its heavy-tread tires. The headlights loom above them, protected behind steel grates. The vehicle is coated with thick plates of armor, and painted like a vintage war plane, with a wide red mouth and sharp white teeth emblazoned on the fenders.

This thing is gross, Clarissa says.

It's equipped for unpredictable and off-road travel, Marie says. It can also seat sixteen people with cargo room to spare. It has mounted weaponry for protection, and carries enough biohazard suits for all sixteen passengers. It's the most appropriate vehicle of the lot.

Marie points at a flame-orange muscle car with an exposed, angry engine block and oversized rear tires. Unless you'd rather drive in that, she says.

They're all gross, Clarissa says.

We'll make do for the time being, Marie says. I'm capable of navigating this vehicle, and Henry, eventually you'll learn to pilot it. For now, collect weapons and food stores. In the event that something goes wrong, I want you children to be provided for.

Can we hear the communications? Clarissa asks.

As they load the vehicle, Marie plays the survivor messages for them.

Ellen's first, Clarissa says.

Hi. This is W9GFO, come back. Uh, anybody who is -- anybody who might still be alive, I hope this comes through. My name is Ellen Cushman. I'm broadcasting on band 17 from a shelter in Temerity. My family is dead. I have spoken to one other person on the CB, but I haven't heard from them in nearly two weeks now. If there are other survivors, I hope you are safe and well. I hope you have supplies. If you are able to get to me, I can help. This shelter is in the second lot on the north side of what used to be Grant Street. The street is mostly gone, so look for an overturned rail car. It's about thirty yards north of the shelter entrance. There's even a bell here. Ring it. Please come. I want to help.

Then Marie plays the new messages.

Is anybody there? I'm Jacob Hiller, and my wife and daughter and I weren't killed in the blast. We're hoping there's someone else alive. We're in a storm shelter and we have a little food, but not enough for more than a few more weeks. We need help, and we can help in return. Please, anyone. Is there anyone there?

This is day four hundred and, oh, I dunno, twenty, maybe? I keep sending out these staticky carrier pigeon messages but nobody ever sends my pigeons back. But alright, whatever, for what it's worth, I'm Harris Samnee, and I have lots of food but no company. I'm in Three Corners, and I play a mean game of chess.

Hello? This seems like a waste of time, but I have to keep trying. My sister and I are survivors, and if anybody else made it, please talk to us. We're kind of going batshit insane down here. We don't even know if it's safe to go out, or if the rest of the world is still there. Hello?

CQ. CQ. This is P6TVN. I guess I'm one of the last ones now. If anybody reads this, respond. Alright, maybe next time. Over.

Marie loops the messages until the vehicle is packed.

Come on, children, she says, holding the door for them.

• • •

The vehicle idles at the base of a long ramp.

Mr. Glass did one thing right, Marie says. The exit provides adequate containment opportunities.

Behind the vehicle, a lumbering steel door churns shut, closing up the armory. Ahead of the vehicle, another steel door rises slowly, revealing a long, paved ascent.

Marie shifts into drive, and the vehicle thrums forward.

I feel like we're about to drive out onto the surface of Mars, Henry says. This feels like a space car.

Like a rover, Clarissa says. I feel that, too.

I hope you've both prepared yourself for what the surface will look like, Marie says. Mars may not be too drastic a comparison.

The children both nod silently.

The second gate halts, and Marie drives the vehicle through. The gate begins to drop behind them. The road angles upward, and the children hold fast to each other and the seats.

Far ahead, the third and final gate rises, a tiny sliver of gray light that grows taller and taller. The ascent is a slow one, the tunnel just wide enough for the vehicle to pass if steered carefully.

I'm nervous, Clarissa says.

Me, too, Henry says.

I understand the concept, Marie says.

She downshifts to handle the climb, and the distant gate draws nearer, and stands fully open. The vehicle rumbles and groans, and the children zip up their protective suits. They breathe through elaborate gas masks.

Clarissa takes Henry's hand.

The vehicle approaches the mouth of the tunnel, then passes through. Its tires grip raw earth, and the children stare through the windows as the vehicle emerges from the disguised tunnel.

The land for miles around is scarred. Buildings have been flattened, crushed and mortared into dust. The sky above is a dismal, unhappy brown, striped with silt and decay.

It's worse than Mars, Henry says. There's nothing left.

There are people left, Clarissa says. There's Ellen. And a funny old man who plays chess.

Henry smiles grimly. Everything's going to be okay?

Children, everything is going to be just fine.

It's a whole big world out there, Clarissa says.

Henry looks at her strangely.

Well, it is, she insists.

I guess.

Marie leans forward and taps the dashboard glass. Oh, my, she says.

What is it? Henry asks, alarmed.

We seem to be out of gas, Marie says.

What? Clarissa says.

Marie smiles. A joke, she says.

Clarissa frowns. That's the worst joke ever.

Henry turns to the window and rests his head against the glass. The stripped landscape scrolls by slowly, trees like scorched matchsticks jutting up at the murky sky. He thinks of his family.

Clarissa rests her head on his shoulder, and he puts his

arm around her. They are the two oldest children who have ever lived.

Marie says, Ellen is expecting us.

Henry nods.

Clarissa drifts into sleep on his shoulder.

The world begins again, as it is known to do.

DEAR READER

Thanks very much for spending your money -- and, more importantly, your time -- on my book, *The Man Who Ended the World*. Writing Steven Glass's twisted little journey from lonely to lethal was startlingly fun -- and it was even more satisfying to give him his comeuppance.

This is a self-published book. This means that I depend greatly on readers to help me find a larger audience. If you enjoyed reading this book, here are a few things you can do to spread the word:

- Rate and review the book on Amazon
- Sign up for my mailing list to find out about new books (jasongurley.com)
- Follow me on Twitter (twitter.com/jgurley)
- Like my Facebook page (facebook.com/ authorjasongurley)
- Check out and share my blog at jasongurley.com
- Read another of my books!

One of the best things about being an independent author is that I'm more accessible to readers than other authors are sometimes able to be. If you bump into me online, say hello. I'd love to hear from you!

Jg

ABOUT THE AUTHOR

Jason Gurley is the author of *Greatfall, The Man Who Ended the World, The Settlers, The Colonists* and *Eleanor*. Born in the squelchy bogs of Texas, then raised in the icy caves of Alaska, he relied on his imagination to keep him warm and dry. As a result, he firmly believes that Superman isn't Superman if he's not wearing red undies, and that Darryl Strawberry had the sweetest swing of all time. He may be the only man alive who believes both, and that's okay.

Jason lives in Oregon with his wife, Felicia, and daughter, Emma Purl, and is a creative director in Portland. He can be found online at **jasongurley.com, facebook.com/authorjasongurley** and **twitter.com/jgurley**, and probably a few dozen other places, if you look hard enough.

Made in the USA
Coppell, TX
18 May 2021

55926343R00154